I0614751

Eugene Browne, F. Ford Rowe

Industrial and Picturesque Rockford

Eugene Browne, F. Ford Rowe

Industrial and Picturesque Rockford

ISBN/EAN: 9783742813749

Manufactured in Europe, USA, Canada, Australia, Japa

Cover: Foto ©Andreas Hilbeck / pixelio.de

Manufactured and distributed by brebook publishing software
(www.brebook.com)

Eugene Browne, F. Ford Rowe

Industrial and Picturesque Rockford

INDUSTRIAL AND PICTURESQUE

ROCKFORD.

COMPILED BY

EUGENE BROWNE AND F. FORD ROWE.

PRICE, 50 CENTS.

POSTAGE ON THIS BOOK, FOUR CENTS.

ROCKFORD, ILL.:
Forest City Publishing Company.
June, 1891.

Original Photographs by
ERICK ERICKSON,
Rockford,   -   -   Illinois.

The Forest City.

The din of commerce greets the listener's ear,
Hammer and anvil sound an echo clear,
The sturdy tread of honest labor's foot
Tells where the oak of progress finds a root.

THE primitive and painted Indian warrior who stood upon the bank of what is now Rock river a trifle over half a century ago, could not have imagined in his wildest hour that child of his could live to see a stately city rise from the prairie and point its hundreds of factory chimneys toward the azure dome. But such a vision became palpable,—and he himself bore reluctant evidence of the first steps toward this wondrous transformation. The white man came, and the red brother abandoned his tepee and disappeared before the wave of civilization.

Now Rockford is a city of thirty thousand progressive people; brimful of business and bustle, and toiling tirelessly. Her citizens are pleased with her past, proud of her present, and fulsome for her future. The fleeting years have made much of her and she stands to-day a queen amid queens and destined for great ends. Men come and go; clouds form and burst; stars rise and fade; but fair Rockford came to stay. Her pulse beats with enduring vigor and the chill of decrepitude can never reach her heart.

It is not the intention of this little book, however, to give an unnatural gloss to her present or future. We deal only in facts; cold, hard realities. The city was settled by sturdy men from New York and New England, and their descendants are here to day. They are not rainbow chasers, fiction fanciers or snake charmers; they are citizens with a world of faith in the prowess of their own right arms. Unaided they have established a wonderful manufacturing municipality. Without soliciting outside capital they have started hundreds of industries whose product foots up many millions every year. They have created a city with broad paved streets, luxuriant homes, unequalled water and sewer systems and perfect fire and police protection: a city where good government and enterprise march hand in hand. The men who have made this rose to blossom are in a position to talk facts. Facts are what they speak to-day. They are talking to you.

WINNEBAGO COUNTY COURT HOUSE.

Past and Present.

———

OCKFORD'S first settlers were Germanicus Kent and Thatcher Blake, who came from Galena in 1835 and built a saw mill on Kent's creek near where the Illinois Central depot now stands. A ford across Rock river was at that place, and hence the name—Rockford. A rope ferry succeeded to the ford, and in 1836 the county of Winnebago was organized with Rockford as the county seat. The territory also included what is now the county of Boone, and at the first election 128 votes were cast. The same area now has a population of over 60,000 souls, half of whom dwell in the city of Rockford, the queen of Northern Illinois.

The first saw mill which marked the city as a manufacturing point has long since disappeared, but 170 other industries have arisen, Phœnix like, and now Rockford lays claim to the title of the industrial city of the west. Against that claim there are none to say her nay. Her dinner pail brigade of eight thousand factory employes forms an argument that cannot be gainsaid.

———

Ten Thousand Worshippers.

———

OCKFORD is a city of churches. There are twenty-seven religious organizations, and at least eight of them own property exceeding in value $50,000 each. Three of the largest and most expensive churches in the state are located in Rockford. The greatest Swedish congregation in the United States is found in the First Lutheran church, which has a membership of 2,300 and can seat them all in their handsome edifice. The Court Street M. E. church has the largest membership of any society of that denomination in the state and worship in a structure costing over $80,000. The Second Congregational society is just completing a $100,000 edifice. St. Mary's Catholic church owns a $75,000 structure and the parish has a membership of 2,200 souls. All the religious denominations are in a prosperous condition and combine a total membership exceeding ten thousand persons. The churches are divided as follows: Baptist three, Catholic two, Christian two, Congregational three, Episcopal one, Lutheran five, Methodist six, Presbyterian three, Unity one. These various societies own church property exceeding $800,000 in value and the edifices have a seating capacity of nearly twenty thousand persons.

The Young Men's Christian Association have a stalwart organization in Rockford and their headquarters is one of the beauty spots in a city of handsome buildings. The association has 300 active members and their building and lot at the corner of State and Madison streets represents an investment of about $80,000.

COURT STREET M. E. CHURCH.

ROCKFORD disclaims the suggestion of being a boom town. She needs no brass band to puff her prowess. The extraordinary growth of the past two years has not been attained by minstrel methods. Her own citizens have expended capital that demanded earnest toil to complete the idea of the investor. Skilled labor accordingly came to her doors and found a ready market. Homes were needed for the new arrivals, and more mechanics were required to build them. Thus the chain lengthened until all branches experienced a wholesome advance. Rockford has doubled her population within a decade, and more than sixty per cent. of this increase has been in the two years ending May 1st 1891. There is no evidence of a cessation. On the contrary never was the city so full of life and promise as at this time. Labor is in strong demand. There are no idle factories, empty stores nor vacant homes in the entire city, and this in spite of the unparalleled building operations that have been and are going on.

The Secret Societies.

THE social side of Rockford claims the admiration of all visitors. Her people are fraternal and hospitable, as becomes a community which traces its ancestry back to the old New England homes. Within her gates are many social organizations in which the stranger finds a cordial greeting. The many secret societies which adorn the social fabric of the nation are widely represented in the city. The Masonic bodies are very strong, as are also the Odd Fellow organizations and Knights of Pythias. The uniformed rank of the latter finds its headquarters here, as also do the Select Knights, the Good Templars and the Grand Circle of White Men. Other organizations are the Elks, the Red Men, the Foresters, the Royal League, the Hibernians, the A. O. U. W., the Royal Arcanum, the Knights of Honor, the Modern Woodmen, and something less than a score of other secret bodies. There are also very many social and literary clubs, assembling for various purposes. Many of these are luxuriantly located and all in flourishing condition. The Thursday Knights, the Y. M. C. U. and the Knights Templar have exceptionally handsome headquarters.

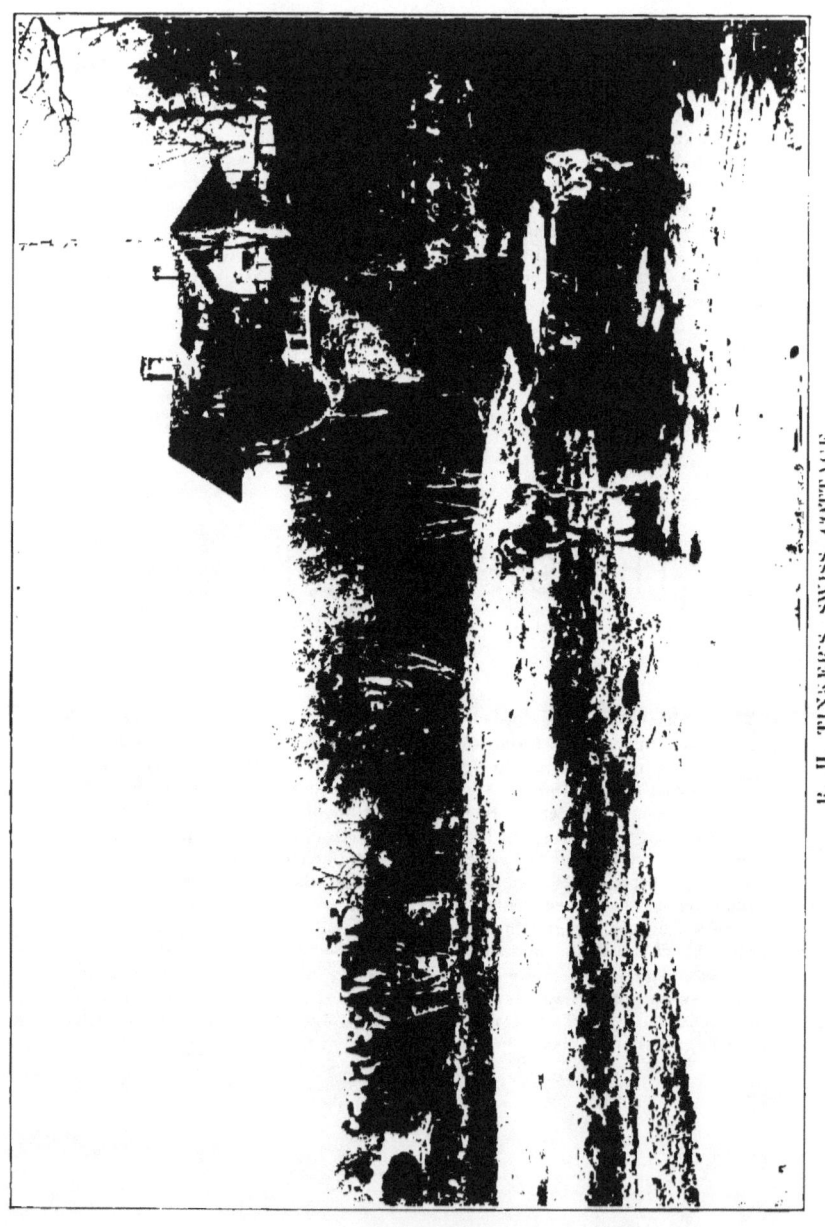

R. H. TINKER'S SWISS COTTAGE.

Education in Rockford.

A N unrivalled opportunity is afforded the young idea to shoot in the city of Rockford. Nothing lies between it and the zenith sun. The municipality supports fourteen large public schools and three annexes, in which all common school branches are taught by competent instructors. Besides this there are the famous Rockford Seminary, the Rockford College, the Rockford Academy and other private schools where general knowledge may be acquired, and also various conservatories and schools of art and music. The census shows a population of over ten thousand souls between the ages of six and twenty-one, and of this number nearly four thousand are duly enrolled in the public schools under seventy-five skilled teachers. The management rests in a board of education and a school committee of the common council. The High school is a magnificent building, occupying a commanding site on the east bank of the river. It was erected at a cost of $40,000. The fourteen schools of the city represent an investment of $250,000 for the buildings and sites. Prof. P. R. Walker is superintendent of schools.

The Rockford Seminary was founded forty-two years ago, and its alumnæ may be found all over the land. Among its graduates are many who have found fame in the various avenues of life that are open to the gentle sex. The buildings are situated in a romantic park of ten acres lying on the river's bank. The property is valued at over $100,000 and the average number of pupils is about 125. Rockford college more especially educates its pupils for a business career, and is a large and flourishing school. A graduate of the Rockford high school is admitted without question or examination into the leading colleges and universities of the country.

Handsome Business Blocks.

C ERTAINLY no more unfailing criterion of the material progress and prosperity of Rockford could be adduced than the number of solid and substantial business houses which have been built; many conspicuous for their artistic architectural design and the completeness of their appointments. Among them might be mentioned the Stewart block, costing $80,000, Perry & Lake block, costing $50,000, Third National Bank and Blake block, costing $40,000, Central block, costing $25,000, Sumner block, costing $25,000, Burpee and Woodruff block, $50,000, Rockford National Bank, $25,000, and the Hutchins & Lake block, $30,000. But while the progress made in 1889 and '90 was remarkable, the present year gives greater promise of an unprecedented activity, as a large number of magnificent buildings are to be started, among which are the new hotel costing $250,000, the Commercial Bank building to cost $150,000, and also the government building to cost $100,000.

ROCKFORD FEMALE SEMINARY.

Pleasures of Summer.

DURING the torrid months of summer and the mellow autumn days the Rockfordite and his visitor from abroad brush away many of the cares of commerce and take advantage of the numerous opportunities afforded for out of door recreation. Rock river, one of the most picturesque streams in the west flows through the city, and its banks are lined with many beauty spots. Picnic and camping parties pitch their quarters above and below the city, and within easy reach; so that the elements are not to be feared. The Rockford Yacht Club was formed last year, and operates the spruce and staunch little steamer Arrow, which plys up and down the river constantly, visiting the recreation parks and camping grounds. The vessel will carry two hundred passengers, and is but one of a numerous fleet of steam and sail craft that plow the picturesque stream. Harlem Park, Remington Park, Riverside, Arrow Park, Latham Grove and Edgewater are some of the superb retreats along the river bank. The former is a part of the river boulevard, and is reached by driveway and electric car, as well as by the stream. It has been converted into an elaborate park, and is utilized for picnics, promenade concerts, encampments, and other out-of-door gatherings. The novel Switchback railroad, or midsummer toboggan, is located here, and is a drawing card for the park. The Fair association have grounds near the center of the city that form a natural amphitheatre. They are illuminated by electricity and devoted to summer night concerts as well as the fair. The property contains a half mile race track, and is used by the city as a public park.

The Rockford Driving Club was organized in the early spring of 1891, with Frank G. Smith, President, H. H. Palmer, Vice President, C. C. Jones, Secretary, and Geo. L. Woodruff, Treasurer. The club owns magnificent grounds, embracing seventy acres, and have laid out a kite-shaped mile track that is pronounced the best and fastest in the west with one exception. The park contains an amphitheatre seating three thousand persons, and all the appointments are patterned from the most approved racing courses of the world. The club gives at least two trotting meetings each year, and offers liberal purses. The grounds are easily accessible by electric cars or the St. Paul road, lying just north of the city limits.

The Rockford Base Ball Club was organized this year, with that crack player and manager, Hugh Nicol, at the helm. The club secured a franchise in the Illinois and Iowa league, composed of eight lively cities. They have a strong team, and their park is located in the west end on the route of the new electric street car line. The club promises to finish a successful season.

Only seven miles from Rockford are the famed Blackhawk Springs. Within easy reach are the many delightful lakes of Southern Wisconsin and Northern Illinois. The city is in the "health belt," and her people need scarcely stir from their doors to seek a fresh and invigorating summer resort. The Ransom Sanitarium, located on the river just north of the city, has quite a reputation as a curative establishment, whether it be the summer or the winter season.

All things considered, Rockford is especially favored in her situation. The blizzards of winter and the extreme sultry days when the dog star rules do not fall to her lot. The climate is even, and the annual rain-fall comparitively small; all of which assists in sustaining the city's claim as a spot for healthful out-door recreation.

ROCKFORD ELECTRIC MANUFACTURING COMPANY'S PLANT.

As a Jobbing Point.

——

ROCKFORD has developed into quite a jobbing center. The same factors which have been instrumental in making her a manufacturing center, are the ones which contribute largely to her success as a jobbing point. The railway facilities are unexcelled. In supplying surrounding towns and cities quite a wholesale and jobbing trade has been established in drugs, groceries, harness, paper, cigars, snuff, meats and seeds, reaching annually into a very handsome sum.

The Commercial Club.

——

ONE of the city's more recent creations is the Commercial Club, formed the present year and already domiciled in a handsome home on North Main street in the stylish residence portion of the city. Their club house possesses perhaps the handsomest interior in the town, the decorations alone costing $3,000. The membership includes fifty or more of the young business men of the city, who find the Club residence a very convenient and attractive spot in which to entertain friends from other cities. The Club is quite a social one and there is a ladies' reception night each week. The officers are: O. P. Trahern, President; E. H. Keeler, Vice-President; Paul F. Schuster, Secretary and Treasurer.

The Water Works.

——

THE water supply of the city is a source of special pride to the citizens and of profit to the municipality. The water works represent an investment of $400,000 on the part of the city, and they yield a handsome revenue each year. The supply comes from five artesian wells, having an average depth of 1500 feet each. The works are fully equipped with the best Holly machinery and the pumps have a capacity of eleven million gallons per diem—enough to supply a city of 75,000 inhabitants. The water is as pure and sparkling as that which flows from a mountain spring. There are forty miles of water mains laid in the city, and many more to follow. There are three hundred public hydrants for fire service. The total pumpage at the works during 1890 was 866,000,000. The revenue of the water department was $27,000 and the operating expenses $11,000. There are no cities in the Union better or more cheaply supplied with water than Rockford. The whole is under the efficient charge of Chas. W. Calkins, chief engineer and superintendent.

FIRST LUTHERAN SWEDISH CHURCH.

Municipal Management.

———

THE affairs of the city are in an enviable condition in spite of the large sums that have been expended for public improvements within the past two or three years. Rockford owns property to the value of a million dollars, and her indebtedness is only $250,000. The assessment is based upon one-tenth to one-fifth of the actual valuation, and the rate of taxation is about three per cent on these figures—much less than in almost every other growing city in the state. Within the past two years the city has expended $125,000 for bridges and $70,000 for paving. There are now fourteen miles of large sewer mains, making an excellent drainage system which is being added to from month to month. The entire business portion of the city is splendidly paved, and two miles more of brick pavement is now being laid in other districts. Electric street railways run to all parts of the city and clear out to all the later factory additions, furnishing rapid and satisfactory communication in every way. The city possesses every metropolitan advantage, and the electric lights that hover over her are not more brighter than her future. The business-like administration of Mayor J. H. Sherratt which witnessed so many permanent municipal improvements, finds a worthy successor in that of Mayor Harry N. Starr.

———

Fire Department.

———

ANOTHER thing that is pardonable in the citizens of Rockford is the amount of pride which they take in the fire department, which has not only a local reputation but is celebrated throughout the state for its efficiency. It is a paid department, and numbers eighteen men. The property consists of one steamer, one mogul, two hose carriages, two hose wagons, one hook and ladder wagon, twelve horses, 3,000 feet of hose, and four engine houses. The value of this property is $38,874.00. Edward Hefferan is chief marshal, succeeding that efficient officer, John T. Lakin. Owing to the promptness and the manner in which the department is handled, we will venture to make the assertion that Rockford has a less number of fires than any city of its size in the state. The city has twenty-four miles of fire alarm telegraph with twenty-eight boxes and seven house stations, affording rapid communication with the factory districts.

Police Protection.

———

AMONG the many things which catch the eye of a stranger upon entering Rockford is its police force, which is composed of as fine and handsome a lot of men as one might see in many a day, and who manage to keep the rougher element in the "straight and narrow way," and thus maintain the reputation which Rockford has as a moral city. The force numbers eighteen men, with Ed. Tisdale as chief.

———

A Railroad City.

———

THE tie that binds—the railroad tie, is one that bisects Rockford at frequent intervals and easily connects her with all the thoroughfares of steel that cover the face of the continent as with a net. The city lies on four great systems of railroad, and is one of the greatest points for travel and shipment that the Mississippi Valley contains. Fifty passenger trains arrive or depart daily, bearing their thousands of travelers to all parts of the land. The city is but a little over two hours' run distant from Chicago, and there are more than a score of luxurious trains running daily between the two points. For the handling of freight the arrangements are perfect. Nearly every one of the two hundred industrial enterprises of the city are connected by sidetrack with some road, and there is a project on foot for the construction of a belt line around the town for the accommodation and advantage of all. Rockford gets the benefit of a low rate on in and out freights, and is so situated that lumber, iron, coal, and all raw materials are quickly and cheaply brought to her doors.

The aggregate of freight handled at Rockford station by all roads is enormous. Mile after mile of trains pass out or in each week, bearing to all the world the story of her prowess as a city of commerce and industry.

THE ILLINOIS CENTRAL.

Perhaps as prime a factor in the city's marvellous growth of recent years was the entrance of the Illinois Central railway into the limits. It cost the company something like a million dollars, but when the work was completed the city began to put on its good clothes and to swell. The company now has nearly five miles of sidetracks and yards in and around Rockford, and a score of large factories have been erected along their right of way, to all of which they have lent their encouragement. Small wonder, then, that the Rockfordite swears by the Central and calls it the godfather of the boom. The main line from Chicago to Sioux City

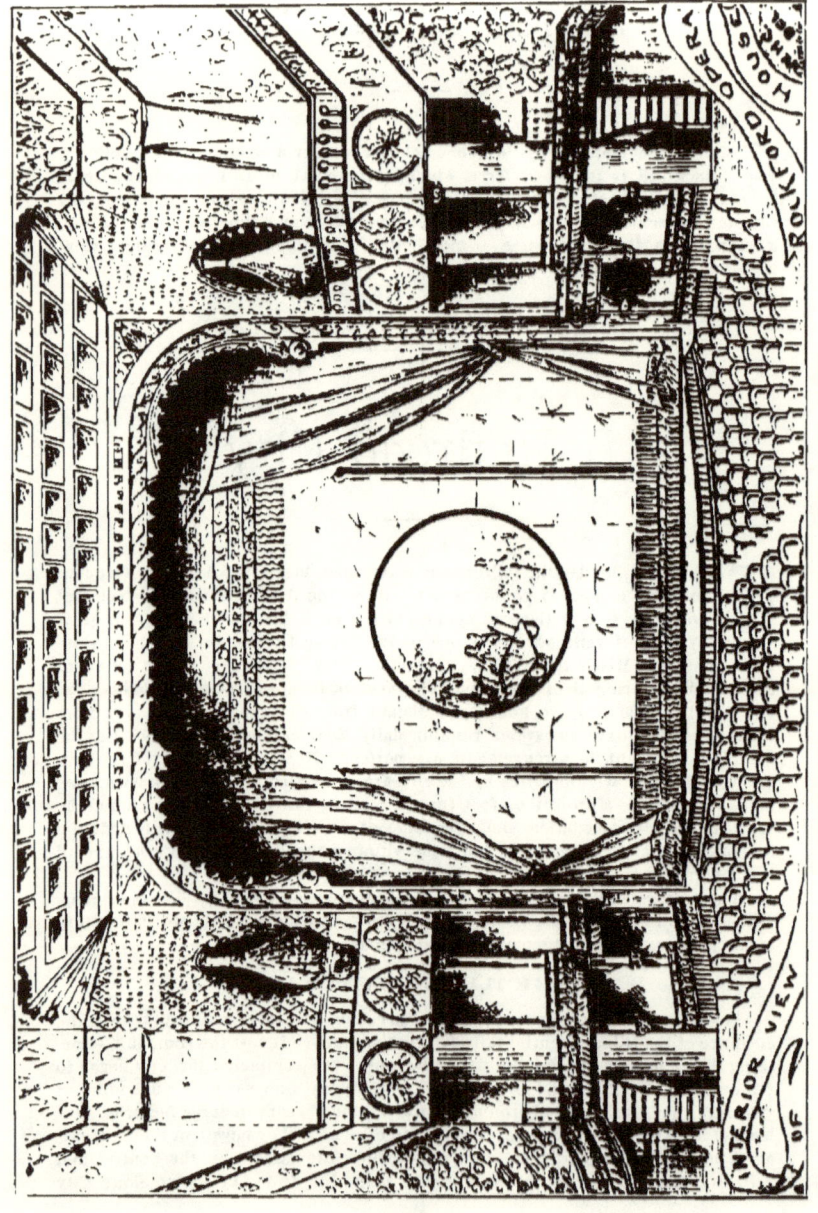

ROCKFORD OPERA HOUSE—INTERIOR VIEW.

passes through Rockford, and the most luxurious and rapid trains in the West pass over it. Two hours has been beaten between Rockford and Chicago, and this division has been pronounced the best piece of railway construction west of New York. Certain and rapid connection with all of the company's 3,000 miles of rail west, east, north, and south is afforded from Rockford, and all trains roll into a palatial passenger station, which is pronounced the greatest beauty spot on the line of any railway in the state. Both the freight and passenger business of the company is enormous, and much is due to the tireless energy and popularity of the general agent at Rockford, Ald. Ed. W. Brown.

"THE BURLINGTON ROUTE" (C. & I. RAILWAY).

Rockford stands as an important point on the mighty Burlington system by virtue of its being the northern terminus of the Chicago & Iowa road, one of the extensive lines included in their operations and controlled entirely by them. The division extends to Aurora, with connections at that place, Shabbona, or Rochelle, with the main Burlington lines in the north and west. The magnificent train service of this great system of steel is a matter of praise on the part of all tourists. For speed, luxury and safety the Burlington trains challenge the universe. Close and certain connections are made to enable the traveler to quickly reach any one of the hundreds of stations on the system, as well as to open the entire railway operations of the land to his accommodation. The local business of the road is very large. Many of Rockford's heaviest shippers are on the right of way, and all have facilities afforded by a complete system of sidetracks. The business, both freight and passenger, continually shows a wholesome increase. Supt. H D. Judson, of the Chicago division, is in charge of affairs at Aurora, and Al. G. Everett is the efficient general agent of the road with headquarters in Rockford There are over 7,000 miles of steel railway directly controlled by the Chicago, Burlington & Quincy system, and all is quickly available from Rockford.

CHICAGO, MILWAUKEE & ST. PAUL.

This system. pronounced the greatest in the world. has an important division passing through Rockford, and a huge business, especially in the way of bringing in lumber from the north, is transacted. Trains run from Madison to Davis Junction, connecting with their main lines east and west, and reaching the thousands of lively stations touched by the company. Their interests here are looked after by J. A. Cotton. The company occupy a passenger station jointly with the C. & I., with Lew Blake as general ticket agent.

CHICAGO & NORTHWESTERN.

One of the greatest, and the pioneer division of this huge system is the 120 miles of track between Freeport and Chicago, and on which Rockford is the leading station. All points on the 7,000 miles of rail controlled by this company can easily and quickly be reached from Rockford by means of the handsome vestibule trains that pass through daily. They do a very large business, both freight and passenger, and their interests locally are in charge of E. E. Manning.

The Field of Finance.

THE numerous banking and financial institutions of the city have always deservedly commanded the confidence of the community. No breath of suspicion or portent of panic has ever dimmed their credit. There are now six national and two state banks. Two others are in process of organization. All are luxuriantly housed and possess every modern safeguard against the attack of the fire fiend. It is easier for a camel to go through the eye of a needle than for a cracksman to enter the strong box of a Rockford bank.

Recent statements made by them are summarized below:

Forest City National Bank. John D. Waterman, President; Paul F. Schuster, Cashier. After but 223 days of business the loans and discounts were $163,263; total resources, $230,223; cash capital, $100,000; deposits, $101,130; surplus, $6,593.27.

Rockford National Bank. Gilbert Woodruff, President; W. F. Woodruff, Cashier. Capital, $100,000; resources, $478,303; surplus and profits, $97,967.

Second National Bank. G. A. Sanford, President; Geo. E. King, Cashier. Capital, $200,000; resources, $837,863; surplus and profits, $93,174.

Winnebago National Bank. T. D. Robertson, President; Chandler Starr, Cashier. Capital, $100,000; resources, $704,648; surplus and profits, $121,989.

Manufacturers' National Bank. C. O. Upton, President; A. P. Floberg, Cashier. Capital, $125,000; resources, $428,690; surplus and profits, $20,422.

Peoples' Bank. A. D. Forbes, President; W. H. McCutchan, Cashier. Capital $125,000; resources, $607,320.50; surplus and profits, $55,593.78.

American Exchange Bank. John Budlong, President; Rob't L. Gillen, Cashier. Capital, $50,000; established 1891.

Third National Bank. A. C. Spafford, President; G. C. Spafford, Cashier. Capital, $80,000; resources. $526,257; surplus and profits, $55,975.

BUILDING AND LOAN ASSOCIATIONS.

Home Building and Loan Association. Seely Perry, President; Geo. F. Penfield, Secretary. Authorized capital, $1,000,000; assets, $346,362; loans in force, $329,245.

Swedish Building and Loan Association. P. A. Peterson, President; Alfred T. Lindgren, Secretary. Capital, $2,000,000; assets, $75,681.85; loans in force, $65,365.40.

Rockford Building and Loan Association. E. H. Keeler, President; S. Fletcher Weyburn, Secretary. Authorized capital, $20,000,000; organized Oct. 1890; assets, $13,824; loans in force, $13,450.

Rockford Security and Investment Company. Daniel Goodlander, President; S. Fletcher Weyburn, Secretary. Capital, $50,000; organized May, 1890.

INSURANCE COMPANIES.

Rockford Insurance Company. John Lake, President; Chas. E. Sheldon, Secretary. Capital, $200,000; assets, $801,488; net surplus, $90,214.

Forest City Insurance Company. Gilbert Woodruff, President; A. H. Sherratt, Secretary. Capital, $100,000; assets, $434,316; net surplus, $88,284.

Manufacturers' and Merchants' Mutual Insurance Company. H. W. Price, President; Geo. S. Roper, Secretary. Assets, $298,564; net surplus, $34,456.

Summary of Facts and Figures

THE citizens of Rockford may well feel proud of the magnificent showing which its industries make, as will be seen by the following facts and figures which have been carefully compiled, and may be relied upon:

Capital invested	$ 6,703,500 00
Annual product	15,439,000 00
Annual pay roll (for same)	4,393,000 00
Making a weekly pay roll in factories alone	83,11232
Actual number of industries	174
Actual number of hands employed	7,893

The Various "Ends."

BY the vast development of the past two years, and the fact that twenty-seven new manufacturing industries have been added to the city within that time have made many an acre into urban property that formerly lay without the pale of the city limits and was largely given over to the peaceful pursuits of agriculture. Of the 750 homes built or being built within the past two years, one-third have been erected on this erstwhile outlying property, and the greatest improvement to the city is here noted. The factories, too, have gone into these new additions, and hence their future is well assured. The North End, the West End, the East End, and the Southeastern additions all clearly demonstrate that the growth of Rockford is regular and certain. All values have greatly advanced, and the city is becoming compactly built up with homes that are far superior to those that any other manufacturing city in the world can boast of.

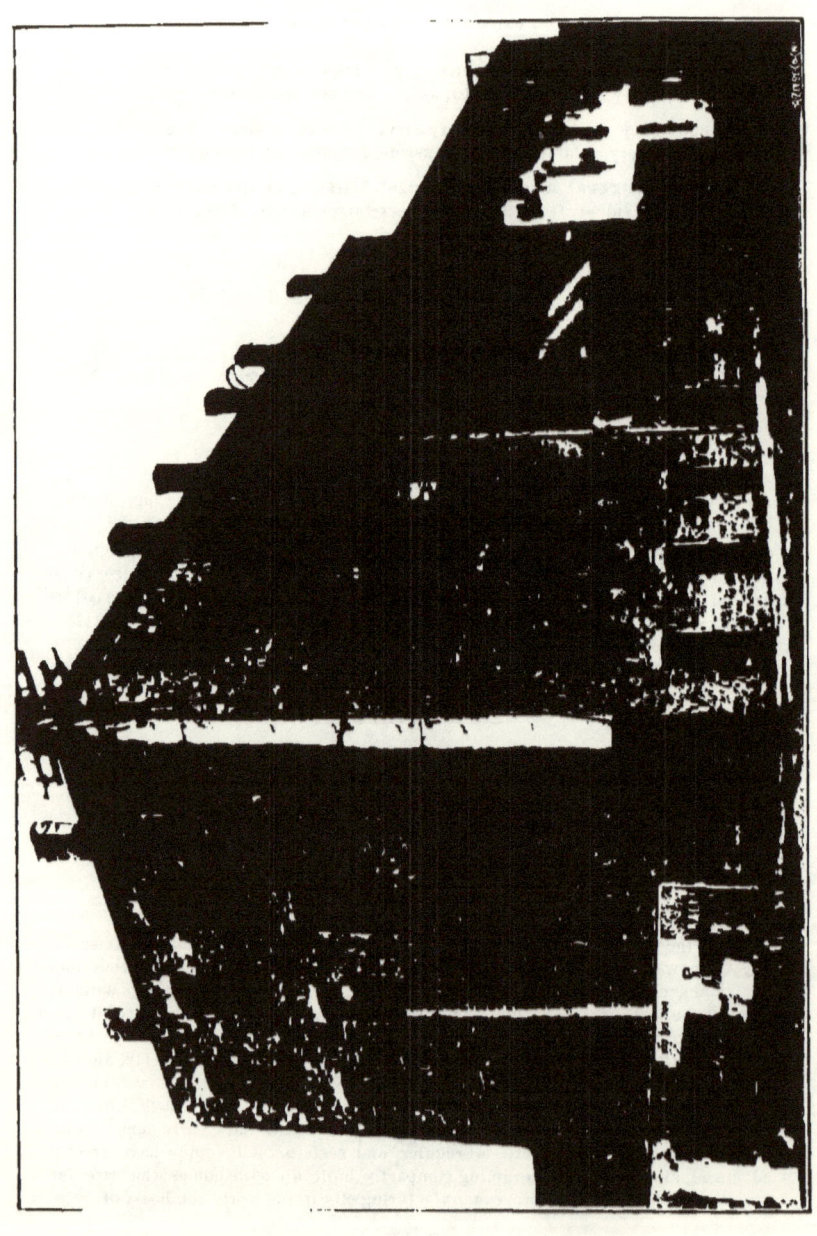

The Co-operative Idea.

I N a score of the largest manufacturing institutions of the city the co-operative plan of conduct prevails. The most insignificant employe possesses his share of stock and feels a lively interest in the business. Such things as strikes or labor troubles are never heard of—neither are there any failures. The feeling between employer and employed is that of mingled interest and division of profit. In no city in the union is this situation more pronounced than in Rockford. Then, too, the great diversity of the city's manufactures place her beyond the reach of market fluctuations or climatic influence. There are no enormous factories in the city where labor troubles may foment or business depression affect an entire community. There are over 600 different articles manufactured in the 174 different industrial institutions of which the city boasts, and hence a disturbance in any particular branch can never bring a tremor to the Rockford pulse. Her industries are as immovable as the hills and as regular as the hour glass.

Industrial Directory.

FURNITURE FACTORIES.

Climax Slide and Table Company. Capital stock, $50,000. B. A. Knight, President; E. R. Lahman, Secretary. Manufactures extension table slides and center tables. Annual output, $50,000; employ forty hands; pay roll $25,000; factory (brick) 36x70, three stories high.

Central Furniture Company. Located at the southeast end of water power; organized in 1878; capital, $125,000. Its present officers are: S. A. Johnson, President; J. R. Anderson, Vice-President; Aug. Peterson, Secretary and Treasurer. They are manufacturers of book-cases, desks and extension tables, and estimate their annual output at $150,000. They employ 140 hands, with an annual pay roll of $75,000. The size of its factories are 40x100, 40x70, 36x102, four stories; and 50x52, two stories high.

Diamond Furniture Company. Formed in March, 1890, succeeding to the business of Fred Bigalow. They manufacture patent office chairs and other similar lines of furniture. The capital stock is $50,000, and the officers are A. F. Judd, President; and Fred A. Dow, Secretary and Treasurer. The company employs fifty hands, with an annual pay roll of $30,000, and turn out a product aggregating $90,000. They are about to build a new factory in Manning's subdivision.

FACTORY OF W. F. & JOHN BARNES CO.

Excelsior Furniture Company. Organized in 1881, with a capital stock of $50,000. The present officers are Thos. D. Reber, President; Aug. Haegg, Vice-President; C. F. Salstrom. Secretary and Treasurer. They manufacture a fine grade of parlor furniture. The annual output is $90,000. They employ seventy-five hands, with an annual pay roll of $35,000. The factory is of brick and wood 60x100 and 80x100, three stories in height, with an engine house 60x20.

Forest City Furniture Company. Rockford's pioneer industry in the furniture line. The business was established in 1869 by A. C. Johnson, and the present company was incorporated in 1875. The officers are: Gilbert Woodruff. President; R. W. Emerson, Secretary and Treasurer; A. C. Johnson, Superintendent. A general line of furniture and office desks is manufactured. The capital stock of the company is $150,000. The plant of the company includes four large four-story brick buildings, with a floor area of 150,000 square feet. They also have six acres of yard room for lumber storage. They employ an average of 240 hands and do a business exceeding $300,000 a year.

Illinois Chair Company. Organized in April, 1891; capital stock of $50,000, with R. L. McCulloch, President; G. E. Knight, Secretary. They will employ 200 hands, with an annual pay roll of $100,000, and estimate their annual output at $200,000. They will manufacture a fine line of chairs. The main building will be of brick 135x65, three stories high, with large warehouse, 80x80, three stories.

Mechanics' Furniture Company. Formed in the spring of 1890, with the following officers: L. M. Noling, President; John Ek, Vice President; Jonas Peters, Secretary; A. P. Floberg, Treasurer; Alfred Kjerner, superintendent. Manufacture a line of hall trees, desks, book-cases and cabinets. Capital, $75,000; employ eighty hands, with an annual pay roll of $40,000, and a product of $125,000. The factory is of brick and frame, located at the corner of Seminary Street and the C. & I. crossing. The building is 80x144 feet in size and four stories high.

Phœnix Furniture Factory. Located at the corner of Fulton and Latham Ave., North End; are manufacturers of chamber suits, extension tables, and chiffoniers: organized July 1st, 1890, with a capital stock of $50,000, with Ed. H. Marsh, President; Geo. Penfield, Vice President; Chas. E. Cohoe, Secretary and Treasurer; employ 100 hands, with an annual pay roll of $36,500; estimated annual output $125,000. The buildings are brick, 128x80, four stories high and a basement, engine room 40x50.

Rockford Burial Case Company. Located corner Peach and Ogden Streets. Capital stock, $75,000. L. B. Williams. President; W. C. Blinn, Vice-President; C. L. Grout. Secretary and Treasurer. Company organized in 1882. They manufacture wood and cloth-finished caskets. Annual product, $75,000; employ thirty hands, with a pay roll yearly of $15.000; factory of brick, 100x50 and 50x50, four stories and basement.

Rockford Co-operative Furniture Company. Located at the corner of Ninth Street and Railroad Avenue. Capital stock, $50,000. Present officers: P. A. Peterson, President; C. A. Hult. Secretary and Treasurer; C. E. Knudson, Superintendent. They manufacture a line of combination and cylinder book-cases, sideboards, tables and office desks; annual output. $175,000; employ 135 hands, with an annual pay roll of $65,000. The factories are of brick, four stories high, 42x110, 50x120, with engine room 42x50.

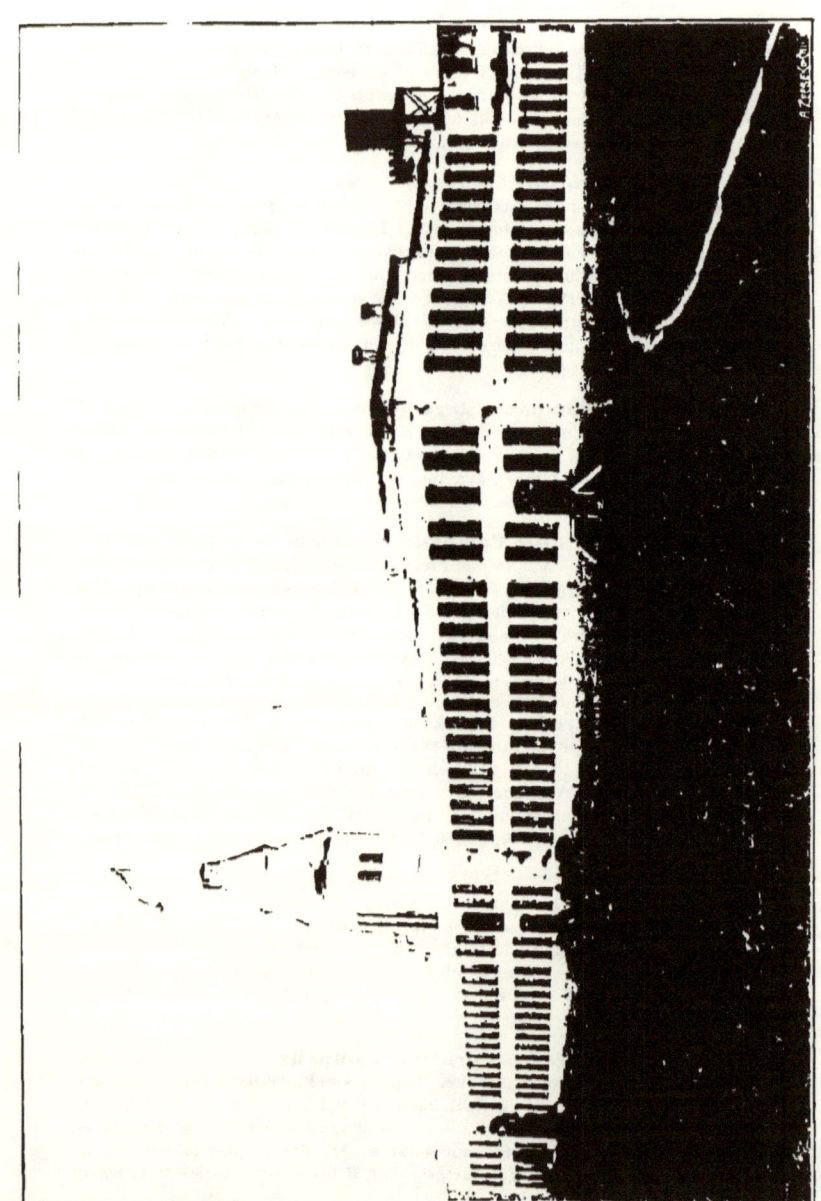

ROYAL SEWING MACHINE COMPANY'S WORKS.

Rockford Chair and Furniture Company. Organized in 1882. Capital, $100,000. The officers are: Andrew Kjellgren, President: Alex. Johnson, Vice-President: Robert C. Lind, Secretary and Treasurer. Located on Railroad Avenue; manufacture a line of book-cases, ladies' desks and fancy furniture. Their plant includes three buildings, 50x150 four stories, 100x100 four stories, and an office and warehouse 50x150, one story high. They employ over 220 hands; annual pay roll, $90,000, and their product exceeds $225,000 yearly.

Rockford Cabinet Company. Organized in 1880, but recently moved to the West End. The capital stock is $50,000. Present officers: Geo. F. Kellogg, President: A. D. Early, Vice President: Chas. H. Porter, Secretary and Treasurer. They manufacture a fine grade of wood mantles, and give employment to 65 hands, with an annual pay roll of $30,000, and produce annually $75,000 worth of goods. The factory is of brick, 64x128, four stories high.

Rockford Desk and Furniture Company. Located on North Second Street, in the Knightville addition. Capital, $50,000. The officers are: A. P. Floberg, President: Robert Bauch, Vice-President: O. Berquist, Secretary and Treasurer. Manufacture a line of desks, secretaries, combination, library and extension tables. Their annual product will aggregate $110,000; employ 115 hands, with an annual pay roll of $55,000. Their factory building is brick veneered, 65x120 feet in size and four stories and basement high.

Rockford Mantel and Furniture Company. Incorporated May 10, 1890, with a capital stock of $100,000. The officers are: Alex. Johnson, President: P. A. Peterson, Vice-President: and Louis Sandine, Secretary and Treasurer. They manufacture a line of mantels and hall trees, and produce annually $150,000 worth of goods: give employment to 125 men, with a yearly pay roll of $75,000. The factory is of brick 82x182, three stories and basement.

Rockford Standard Furniture Company. Located on Railroad Avenue. Capital stock, $75,000. Officers: J. A. Lundgren, President: P. H. Palmer, Vice-President and Superintendent: D. R. Peterson, Secretary and Treasurer. The company was organized in 1887, and manufactures a line of sideboards, book-cases, cabinets and secretaries; employ 185 hands; annual product, $150,000, with an annual pay roll of $65,000. Their plant includes two large four-story brick veneered buildings, respectively 66x125 and 97x115 feet in size.

Rockford Union Furniture Company. Organized in 1876. Capital and surplus, $100,000. Its present officers are: C. F. Anderson, President: C. F. Blomberg, Vice-President: and P. A. Peterson, Secretary and Treasurer. They are manufacturers of ladies' cabinet book-cases and pillar tables, and do an annual business of over $250,000 per year: employ 250 hands, with an annual pay roll of $125,000. The factory is of brick 80x176 and 128x160, three stories high.

Skandia Furniture Company. Located on North Third Street, and manufacture a line of hall-trees, book-cases, cylinder desks, secretaries and pillar extension tables. The company was organized in 1889, with a capital stock of $75,000. Present officers: P. A. Peterson, President: G. Flodell, Vice-President: W. A. Brolin, Secretary and Treasurer. They produce annually $150,000 worth of goods, and give employment to 150 hands, with a pay roll of $72,000 per year. The buildings are of brick, 64x128 and 64x128, four stories and a basement high.

NATIONAL SYRUP CO.'S SUGAR WORKS.

Star Furniture Company. Located at corner of Eighteenth Avenue and Fourteenth Street; manufacturers of combination book and library cases, hall trees. Capital stock, $100,000. Its present officers are F. G. Hogland, President; Anthony Stenholm, Vice-President; Aug. P. Floberg, Treasurer; P. G. Lundquist, Secretary; G. L. Wenerstrom, Superintendent. They employ 140 hands, with an annual pay roll of $60,000; annual product, $125,000; factory is built of brick 80x160, four stories high, and it is their intention to build this summer a warehouse 80x160, four stories high.

West End Furniture Company. Located corner of Factory Street and Johnson Avenue; organized July 7, 1890, with a capital stock of $50,000. Present officers are: B. A. Knight, President; O. W. Haegg, Vice President and Secretary; Paul Schuster, Treasurer. They are manufacturers of book-cases, side-boards, hall-trees, tables and chiffoniers; give employment to 150 hands, with an annual pay roll of $80,000, and estimate their output at $200,000 per year. The factory is 80x144, five stories and basement high, and built of brick.

AGRICULTURAL IMPLEMENTS.

The W. F. & John Barnes Company. The business was first estab-lished in 1871, and the present corporation formed in 1884. The officers are W. Fletcher Barnes, President; B. Frank Barnes, Vice-President; and John Barnes, Secretary and Treasurer. Their buildings are located at the corner of Water and Oak Streets, in East Rockford, and the company manufacture foot, hand and steam power machinery for wood and iron working; lathes, drills, saws, emery grinders, and various specialties. They have an average of 175 employes on their pay-roll. Their main building is of brick, four stories high. The company occupy a total of nearly an acre of floor area.

H. B. Busing & Company. Located Race Street, water power; manu-facturers of N. C. Thompson sulky cultivators, hay-rakes, lever harrows, plow jointers and coulters; amount of capital invested $3,000. They employ twelve hands, with an annual pay-roll of $3,000. Annual output, $15,000; occupy two top floors, 80x120, of N. C. Thompson building.

Emerson, Talcott & Co. This concern is one of Rockford's oldest and most reliable firms, having been first established in 1852; incorporated in 1876. They manufacture agricultural implements, and produce annually, almost one mil-lion dollars' worth of their goods, and give employment to 350 hands, with an annual pay-roll of $225,000. The factories cover two and one half acres of ground.

Forest City Bit and Tool Company. This firm is located on Kish-waukee Street, and has a capital stock of $25,000. Its present officers are L. M. Noling, President; A. J. Anderson, Vice-President; Aug. Floberg, Treasurer; Oscar J. F. Larson, Secretary. They manufacture a full line of bits and wood boring tools, and produce annually $50,000 worth of their goods; employ twenty-five hands, with an annual pay-roll of $15,000. The factory is of brick, 40x100, three stories high.

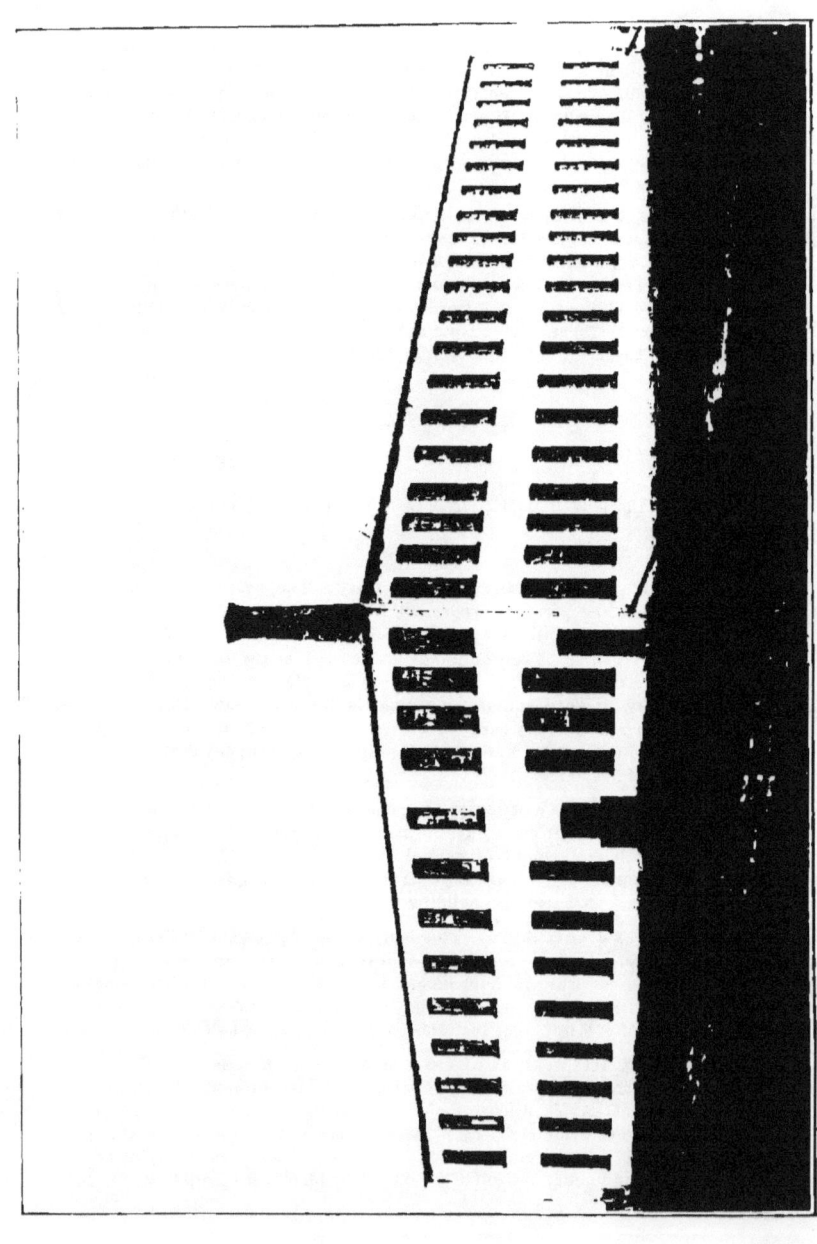

Jones, Woodruff & Co. The manafacture of pumps, windmills and electric fire alarms is carried on at Nos. 117 and 119 South Court Street, and was established in 1874. A capital of $25,000 is invested in the business, and an average of fifteen hands are employed. The business transacted will aggregate $40,000, with an annual pay-roll of $6,000. The buildings occupied are of frame, one 22x70, two stories, and the other, 22x50, one story high.

Rockford Bolt Works. Located on Mill Street. Capital stock, $20,000; company was organized in 1877. The officers are: S. B. Wilkins, President; R. H. Tinker, Vice-President; C. R. Wise, Secretary and Treasurer. They employ sixty hands, with an annual pay roll of $40,000. The business runs up annually into six figures. The building is of stone, 80x200, two stories high.

Rockford Manufacturing Company. Authorized capital, $200,000. John A. Johnson, President; L. M. Noling, Vice-President; Aug. P. Floberg, Treasurer; August Lind, Secretary: incorporated 1889; manufacturers of agricultural implements; employ sixty hands, with an annual pay-roll of $25,000; factory, 220x 175, two stories.

Rockford Neckyoke Works. C. Eugene Sovereign is proprietor, and manufactures neckyokes, axle washers, carriage top dressing, harness soap, and other specialties, occupying part of the four-story stone building, 50x150 feet in size, located at 640 South Main Street. The capital invested is about $10,000. An average of twelve hands are employed, with a pay-roll of $7,000, and an annual product of $25,000. The business was established in 1880.

Rockford Plow Company. The present company was incorporated in 1883, with a capital of $125,000. The officers are E. L. Woodruff, President; B. A. Knight, Vice-President; T. M. Carpenter, Secretary and Treasurer. The company's plant is located on Mill Street, on the water power, and includes a main building built of stone, 50x140 feet in size, and four stories high. There are six other buildings for warehouse and finishing purposes. The company employs an average of seventy-five men, and does an annual business of $200,000. Their pay-roll averages $80,000, and they manufacture plows, planters, cultivators, seeders and other agricultural implements.

Shoudy Manufacturing Company. The business is conducted by Israel Shoudy, with an invested capital of $10,000, and was established in 1888. Tank heaters, feed cookers, grinders, lawn mower attachments, and all other specialties are manufactured, with a force of ten employes. The business will foot up to $10,000 a year, with a pay-roll of $3,000. The building occupied is on South Wyman Street, on the water power, is of frame, 30x60, two stories high, with a 30x40 wing.

The Skandia Plow Company. Located at the corner of Cedar and South Court Streets. The capital stock is $125,000. The present officers and directors are: P. A. Peterson, President: John Peterson, Vice-President: J. A. Lundgren, Secretary and Treasurer. They manufacture a line of gang and sulky plows, corn planters, check-rowers, harrows and cultivators. Annual product, $200,000, and employs eighty-five hands, with an annual pay-roll of $42,000. Factory 45x100 and 40x100, three stories high, with blacksmith shop 60x120, and warehouse 50x100.

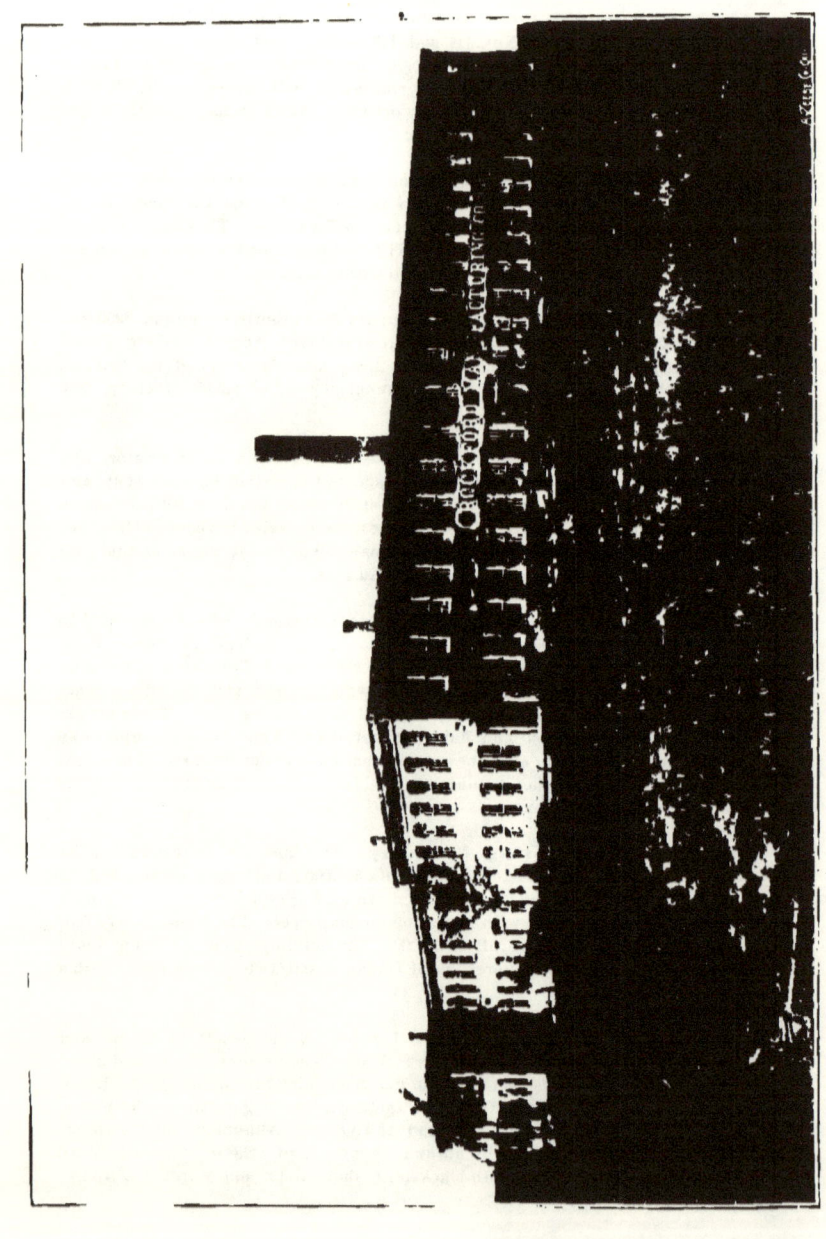

Trahern Pump Company. This is one of Rockford's strongest institutions. The business was originally established in the 60's, but was reincorporated in 1888, with O. P. Trahern as President and John A. Lewis, Secretary and Treasurer. The capital paid in is $120,000, and the company manufactures a complete line of iron and brass pumps, employing from eighty to one hundred hands the year round. Their plant is located at the corner of Wyman and Mill Streets, on the water power, and embraces a three-story stone machine shop, 42x62; a one-story stone foundry 40x115; a five-story brick office and warehouse 30x100; a two-story iron warehouse, 45x40, and a brass foundry of brick, 25x60 feet in size and three stories high.

Utter Manufacturing Company. This concern is located on both sides of Race Street on the water power. The capital stock of the company is $75,000, and the officers are: H. B. Utter, President; E. M. Utter, Vice-President; J. M. Fraley, Secretary and Treasurer. The business was first established in 1848, and incorporated in 1876. The company employs an average of fifty hands in the manufacture of seeders, cultivators, and a general line of agricultural implements. Their plant includes a machine shop and foundry, of stone, one and three stories high and 42x120 feet in size; a pattern and blacksmith shop, of brick, 30x120 feet and three stories high; also five warehouses, embracing about 25,000 feet of total floor area.

Ward Pump Company. This company was organized in 1889, with a capital stock of $5,000. Its present officers are: Frank Ward, President; G. H. Stanley, Vice-President; F. Lane, Secretary; M. E. Ward, Treasurer. They manufacture a full line of iron pumps and cylinders, and produce annually $50,000 worth of goods, giving employment to forty men, with an annual pay-roll of $20,000. The factory is of brick and wood, covering an acre of ground.

The L. A. Weyburn Company. This incorporation was formed in 1885, with L. A. Weyburn as President, and Geo. S. Briggs, Secretary. They manufacture blacksmiths' supplies, live shrinkers, screen doors and hardware novelties, and occupy several buildings on the water power. Their capital stock is $20,000, and they do a business nearly, if not quite, aggregating $100,000 per annum. They employ an average of thirty-five hands, with an annual pay-roll of $18,000. Their main building is 50x140, built of stone.

A. W. Woodward. The business was established in 1872, and a line of water wheel governors and machinery specialties is made. The capital invested is about $7,000. Three employes are at work, and the pay-roll aggregates $2,000, with an annual product of $8,000. The building is located on Mill Street, on the water power, is of wood, 25x50 feet in size, and two stories high.

MACHINE SHOPS AND METAL WORKERS.

Charles Andrews & Co. The Andrews wire works was first established in 1885, and in December 1890 removed to their new building in the West End. All kinds of wire goods are turned out, and the business represents an investment of $6,000. An average of fifteen hands are employed with a pay roll of $5,000 and an annual output footing up to over $10,000. There are two frame buildings, one 30x90 two stories, and the other 15x20 one story high.

H. G. Dickinson & Co. They are located on Race street, water power, and do a general jobbing and repair business of all kinds of machinery. They employ four hands with an annual pay roll of $2,500, and estimate their annual business at $4,000.

A. Hammill. The business of this brass foundry was established in 1890 in a one story brick and frame building 20x100, located on Forbes street, on the water power. Small brass castings are made, and the business will foot up to $2,500 a year.

The Ingersoll Milling Machine Company. Located in Edgewater Addition; organized, April 1891, with capital stock of $80,000. The officers are: Winthrop Ingersoll, President; R. L. McCulloch, Secretary; W. H. McCutchan, Treasurer. They manufacture a line of iron milling machinery, and estimate their annual output at $125,000. They employ one hundred hands with an annual pay roll of $50,000. The factory is of brick. 150x50, two stories high.

Lillibridge & Eibach. Are located on Race street, water power; capital invested $6,000. They do all kinds of repairing in brass and metals, and also bicycles. They employ twenty hands with an annual pay roll of $7,200, and do a yearly business of $18,000. Factory is of wood, two stories high. 30x60.

Love Manufacturing Company. This corporation was formed in 1891 with a capital of $10,000, and does a general machine shop business both in iron and wood, and also conduct a foundry for light and heavy castings. Their machine shop is of frame, 40x50 feet in size and two stories high; the foundry is 50x125, one story. The company employs thirty five hands, with an annual pay roll of $20,000; the business of the concern during the year will foot up to $50,000.

Manny Lemon Juice Extractor Company. This company is located at 106 North Church street, and manufactures a novelty in the shape of a glass extractor which has met with good success, and the firm are doing a nice business annually. Its officers are: Wm. A. Talcott, President; Wm. Lathrop and Jno. P. Manny, Vice-Presidents; Miss J. C. Lathrop, Secretary and Treasurer. The company was organized in October, 1890, with a capital stock of $25,000.

Munson Manufacturing Company. The company was formed in August 1890 with a capital of $3,000. A. M. Munson is President, George S. Briggs, Vice-President, and L. A. Weyburn, Secretary. They occupy a one story frame building, 40x70, located on South Wyman street on the water power. The company manufacture barb wire, employing three men and turning out a product of $18,000 a year. The pay roll is about $1,500 per annum.

Barney McCarren Boiler maker; capital invested $4,000; employs five hands with annual pay roll of $3,500; annual product $15,000.

The Rockford Brass Works. Do a general jobbing business of bronze and brass castings. Located on Mill street, water power; capital stock $10,000. B. E. Trahern, President; F. B. Trahern, Treasurer; and H. Trahern, secretary. The company was organized in 1890; annual product $30,000, employing ten hands; the annual pay roll amounts to $3,600; size of factory 25x50, three stories high, built of brick.

Rockford Electrical Manufacturing Company. The company is located at the corner of Grant and Fulton avenues; the capital stock is $100,000. Its present officers and directors are; C. M. Haven, President; E. A. Van Wie, Secretary and Treasurer; and Geo. A. Mayo, Superintendent. They manufacture arc and incandescent dynamos and motors and railway generators. They give employment to eighty-five hands, with an annual pay roll of $22,000, and produce yearly $150,000 worth of goods. The factory is built of glass and wood and is 50x250 with L 24x48 and engine house 10x24, one story high.

The Rockford Machine Company. Is located at 904 Tenth street; has a capital stock of $10,000; incorporated in 1889. Its present officers are: Chas. A. Forsburg, President and Superintendent; W. F. Noling, Secretary and Treasurer. They are manufacturers of special machinery for wood work; they do an annual business of $15,000, and give employment to twelve hands, with an annual pay roll of $6,000. The factory is 22x65, one story high.

Rockford Malleable Iron Works. The business of this concern was first established in 1854, but the present company was not incorporated until 1880. A. D. Forbes is President, Harry F. Forbes, Secretary; and George Forbes. Superintendent. The company turn out malleable iron castings and their capital stock is $75,000. They occupy several brick, stone and frame buildings at the corner of Mill and Forbes streets on the water power, covering an area of 25,000 square feet, one and two stories high. These buildings were largely rebuilt in 1885. The company employ an average of seventy-five hands with an annual pay roll of about $32,000, and do a business aggregating $100,000 per annum.

The Rockford Steam Boiler Works. Jas. McCarren, proprietor Capital invested $4,000; does a general business as boiler-maker and repair work amounting to $15,000 per year; employs five hands with an annual pay roll of $3,900; the shop is 40x80, one story high and built of brick.

Rockford Tack Company was organized in 1874; capital stock $40,000. Its present officers are: H. W. Price, President; Levi Rhoades, Vice President; Elias Cosper, Secretary and Treasurer; Harry Cosper, Superintendent. The articles manufactured are tacks and small nails. They employ forty hands; annual pay roll $2,200. The present factory was built in 1877 and is composed of stone, being 40x90, three stories high, with an L 30x84 two stories high. They do a business annually of $100,000; their goods are shipped to all parts of the country.

James Rogers. The Rockford Galvanizing Works were bought by the present proprietor in March, 1890, and are located on Race street, on the water power. The capital invested is $2,500; four hands are employed and the business foots up to $5,000 a year. The building occupied is a frame structure 20x40 feet in size and two stories high; the annual pay roll is about $2,000.

ST. MARY'S CATHOLIC CHURCH.

John Spafford & Co., manufacture all kinds of wire goods: John Spafford sole proprietor; capital invested $3),0)); established since 1876; employs twelve hands with an annual pay roll of $9,600; annual output $20,000. The factory is located at 201 and 203 North Madison street; size of factory 42x80, three stories and basement; structure of stone.

Savage & Love. This firm have a general machine shop and pattern-making industry occupying the first floor of the four story stone building at 649 South Main street. They have an invested capital of $10,000 and do an annual business of $25,000; they employ fifteen hands with an annual pay roll of about $7,500. Their establishment is 50x100 feet in size, and the firm have been doing business since 1878.

Spengler Brothers. This firm opened a machine shop and oxydized brass business February 1st, 1891. They occupy the second floor of a three story frame building 40x110 located on Race street, on the water power; their capital invested is about $4,000; they will employ about twelve hands with an annual pay roll of about $6,000 and a business of $20,000 per annum.

Taylor & Worsley. Do general jobbing and repair of iron work. Capital invested $2,000; organized Dec. 1st, 1890, and are located on Race street, water power; estimated out-put, $8,000; employ two hands; size of shop 40x60, one story,

Union Foundry and Machine Company. Located on Cedar street, and do a jobbing business of all kinds of ironcastings; capital invested $25,000; Geo. Peterson & Sons, proprietors. They employ thirty hands, with an annual pay roll of $16,800; annual output $40,000; foundry of wood, two stories high, 70x90.

The Van Wie Gas Stove Company. This company is another of Rockford's latest acquisitions, having moved here from Cleveland, Ohio, in September 1890. They manufacture gas heating and cooking stoves and their appliances; have a capital stock of $40,000, with the present officers: P. G. Van Wie, President; Geo. S. Roper, Vice-President; Geo. D. Roper, Secretary and Treasurer. They employ seventy-five hands at an annual outlay of $30,000, and estimate their annual output at $200,000. The factory is of brick, two stories high, and is located at the corner of Van Wie street and Huffman Boulevard; size of building 3 40x318.

TRAHERN PUMP WORKS.

ROCKFORD TACK COMPANY PLANT.

Forest City Knitting Co. This company was organized in November 1890, with a capital stock of $60,000, with Wm. Nelson, President; Oscar Nelson, Vice-President; F. F. Nelson, Secretary and Treasurer. They manufacture a line of fine ladies' and gentlemen's cotton hosiery, and produce annually over $200,000 worth. They employ one hundred hands, with an annual pay roll of $25,000. The factory is of brick, two stories high, 200x39, with an L 106x39.

Globe Clothing Company. This concern is located at the corner of Sixth Street and Eleventh Avenue, and was incorporated December 13, 1889, with a capital of $50,000. The directors are: August Lundberg, President; C. A. Gustafson, Vice-President; Axel Rydberg, Secretary; Aug. P. Floberg, Treasurer; C. J. Dahlin, Gust Lindblade, Gust Holm, Levin Eksell, directors. They employ forty, five hands, with an annual pay-roll of $13,500, and their product will foot up to $75,000. Their building was erected in 1890, is built of brick, 57x100 feet in size and three stories high.

Graham Cotton Mills. This company was organized in 1865. The capital stock is $150,000, with G. A. Sanford, President; and Freeman Graham, Jr., Secretary and Treasurer. They manufacture carpet warp, cotton towels, cotton batten, and seamless socks, and produce annually $450,000; employ 145 hands, with an annual pay-roll of $60,000. They occupy three large factories on the water power. The company also have large cotton and paper mills at Rock Island, employing 600 hands.

The Nelson Knitting Company. Located on water power. This company was organized in 1880. The capital stock is $160,000. Antes Ruhl, Secretary and Treasurer. They manufacture a line of seamless cotton hosiery, and manufacture over 1,500,000 dozen pairs annually. The factories cover two acres of ground. They employ 400 hands, and do a business of over $800,000 a year.

Henry W. Price, Glove Works. Business established in 1862; located corner of Wyman and Peach Streets, in two three-story frame buildings; manufacture tanned leather gloves; product of factory, $200,000; total business, $500,000 a year; employ 140 hands, with an annual pay-roll of $75,000.

Rhoades, Utter & Co. This is a corporation formed in 1880, and succeeding to the paper mill and jobbing business of Rhoades & Utter, established in 1865. The officers are: Levi Rhoades, President; C. M. Utter, Vice President; and M. B. St. John, Secretary and Treasurer. They manufacture seven tons of straw wrapping paper a day, footing up to $46,000 a year. They employ thirty hands, with an annual pay-roll of $15,000. Their plant is located on Mill Street, on the water power. They occupy three buildings: one two story and basement, frame, 40x64; one two story and basement, stone, 40x62; one one-story frame warehouse, 35x65.

Rockford Linen Fibre Company. Organized June 1891. Capital stock $100,000. Will manufacture paper pulp in the Keeney paper mill plant; will employ about forty hands, with an annual pay-roll of $22,000. They estimate their annual product at $200,000.

H. H. PALMER & CO., CHURN FACTORY.

INGERSOLL MILLING MACHINE CO. (1891).

Rockford Clothing Company. This concern was formed in 1887. The officers are Antes S. Ruhl, President; A. D. Early, Vice-President; and A. L. Brearley, Secretary and Treasurer. The capital stock is $30,000, and the company manufactures men's clothing to order and for the jobbing trade. They employ nearly one hundred hands, with an annual pay-roll of $30,000, and do a business aggregating $150,000 a year. Their building is of brick, two stories high, located at the corner of Church and Chestnut Streets. It was built in 1888, is 32x132 feet in size, with an extensive wing.

Rockford Mitten and Hosiery Company. Located on South Wyman and Cedar Streets. They are manufacturers of woolen mittens and hosiery, with a capital stock of $150,000. The company was organized in 1881, but was reorganized in 1885. The officers are: Wm. Ziock, President and Treasurer; W. A. Talcott, Vice-President;W. H. Ziock, Secretary; directors—Wm. Ziock, W. A. Talcott, W. H. Ziock, Ralph Emerson, Wm. Walton, Oscar Nelson, and A. S. Ruhl. They employ 145 hands, with an annual pay-roll amounting to $42,000. The annual product is $200,000. The building is 180x180, three stories high, the structure being frame.

S. B. Wilkins Company. Manufacture full line of yarns and hosiery, at corner of South Wyman and Cedar Streets; company organized January 1, 1884, with a paid up capital of $150,000. The officers are S. B. Wilkins, President; John W. Hart, Secretary and Treasurer; Geo. S. Wilkins, Assistant Secretary and Treasurer; employ 300 hands, with an annual pay-roll of $90,000. Value of yearly product aggregates $450,000. Buildings are of brick and wood, two and three stories high, and include 35,000 square feet of floor area. They were built in 1881 for S. B. Wilkins & Co., who were succeeded by the present corporation.

Rockford Overall Manufacturing Company. Located 640 South Main Street. Levi Rhoades, President; B. F. Lee, Vice President; Geo. L. Irvine, Secretary and Treasurer. This firm make a general line of working men's goods, consisting of overalls, pants, jackets, shirts, etc.; employ seventy hands; factory, 50x150, two floors.

Rockford Suspender Company. (Successors to J. N. Faust). Company was incorporated January 1, 1891, with a capital stock of $20,000. Its present officers are D. F. Sullivan, President; J. F. Ogilby, Vice-President; J. N. Faust, Secretary and Treasurer. They are manufacturers of suspenders, braces and hose supporters. They employ thirty hands, with an annual pay-roll of $15,000, and estimate their annual output at $120,000; size of factory, 40x80, one floor, and located corner of North Madison and Market Streets.

Rockford Woolen Mills Company. The business was first established in 1863 by John and William Dyson. The present company was incorporated in 1883, and the officers are: R. P. Lane, President; Jeremiah Davis, Vice President; William Dyson, Secretary and Treasurer. They manufacture wool. flannels, yarns and shawls. They have about forty operatives, turning out a product of $40,000 a year, with a pay-roll aggregating $15,000. Their plant includes three buildings. Their main structure is 32x62, four stories high; machine room 30x50, three stories; warehouse 25x50, two stories. All are of frame and located on Mill Street, on the Water Power.

Henry Ulrici. The business of manufacturing paper boxes was established in 1864, and is now conducted in a two-story and basement frame building, 40x100 feet, built in 1887, and situated at No. 1008 Mulberry Street. The capital invested in the business is about $8,000, and an average of twenty hands are employed.

SKANDIA SHOE COMPANY FACTORY.

ROCKFORD BURIAL CASE COMPANY FACTORY.

Royal Sewing Machine Company. This company is one of Rockford's greatest factories. The company was organized July 1890, and commenced operation February 1, 1891. Its capital stock is $100,000, with officers as follows: John Budlong, President; P. A. Peterson, Vice-President; S. S. Budlong, Treasurer; Jno. A. Bowman, Secretary. They employ 200 hands, with an annual payroll of $120,000, and estimate their annual product at $1,000,000. The factory is of brick, and one of the few which have made any attempt at architectural beauty. It is 544x44. two stories high, with engine room, 30x62.

W. W. Swinyer. Manufactures rubber stamps and office novelties, rear of post-office. The business was established in 1883; occupies two rooms in a three-story brick building. Employs three hands. Invested capital, $1,000. Annual product. $5,500.

J. E. Atchison. Capital invested. $3,500. Employs seven hands, with a pay-roll annually of $3,000; product, $7,000; does a general carriage business and wagon trade.

O. E. Burrows' cigar factory is at 220 South Main Street, occupying part of a three-story brick block. Five men are employed, with an annual product of $10,000. The pay-roll runs about $3,500 per annum.

R. Anglemire. Located on North Wyman Street; manufacturer of boots and shoes; established since 1873. Capital invested, $15,000; employs thirty hands, with an annual pay-roll of $15,000; produce yearly $40,000. Factory 23x50. three stories high, and built of stone.

Avery Building and Moving Company. This company do a general moving business. Capital stock, $10,000; C. M. Avery, President; Chas. Shedd, Secretary. They employ during the season from fifty to two hundred men, with an annual pay-roll of $15,000, and do an annual business of $35,000.

Air Brush Manufacturing Company. Located at 119 and 127 North Main Street. This company was organized in April 1883, and its capital is $50,000, with the following officers: L. Walkup, President; L. B. Gregory, Vice-President; W. W. Bennett, Secretary and Treasurer; Will Bennett, Assistant Secretary. They manufacture Mr. Walkup's patent air brush, pantagraphs, etc., and do nickel plating. Twelve hands are employed, with an annual pay-roll of $5,500. The company does a business of $20,000 a year, and occupies the second story of a handsome brick building, 80x100 feet in size. An art school for air brush students is connected.

A. L. Bartlett. Elevator, feed mill and warehouse, No. 500 Cedar Street. Business established in 1856. Capital invested, $20,000. Main building built 1870, 30x50 feet in size. Three warehouses also connected. Main buildings of wood and iron, two stories high. Employs seven hands, with an average annual pay-roll of $4,000. The average business in the manufacturing line aggregates $25,000.

— 41 —

J. G. Chick Milling Company. This company was incorporated in January 1880, with a capital of $100,000. The officers are J. G. Chick, President; F. A. Chick, Vice-President; J. B. Antes, Secretary; F. L. Chick, Treasurer. They manufacture all kinds of flour and feed, and do an annual business of $350,000, employing twenty-five hands, with an annual pay-roll of $15,000. The mill was first built in 1854, since which date several additions have been added.

Blakeman & Dobson Manufacturing Company. The business was established in 1880 by Blakeman & Dobson, who incorporated under the present title in 1883. Benjamin Blakeman is President and Wm. Dobson Secretary of the company. They operate a planing mill and manufacture barrel churns. The capital stock is $30,000, and they employ an average of fifty hands, with a pay-roll of $25,000. They do a business of $90,000 a year. Their plant is located at the corner of Pleasant and Cedar Streets. Their main building is 50x80 feet in size, and a machine room 40x70; both buildings are four stories high.

The Brown Brick Company. This company has a capital stock of $10,000. Its present officers are Sam'l Ennett, President; C. J. Jones, Secretary. They manufacture a line of fine white brick. Annual product, $15,000; give employment to twenty employes, with an annual pay-roll of $9,360.

Connors' Lime Kiln. John Connors, Proprietor. He has $8,000 capital invested, and employs fourteen hands, with an annual pay-roll amounting to $7,200, and does an annual business of $18,000.

S. B. Hendricks conducts a planing mill on Race Street on the water power, and also manufactures wooden water tanks. The business was established in July 1891, with an investment of $4,000. A business of $10,000 a year is now being done by an average of eight employes, and a pay-roll of $3,500. The mill building is 60x100, with stuccoed exterior, and is one story high.

Hess & Hopkins' Leather Company. Tannery located at foot of Acorn Street; office and warehouse, 515 West State Street. Business first established in 1875; present company incorporated in 1882, with a capital of $50,000. Samuel N. Jones, President; L. M. Hess, Vice-President; T. F. Hopkins, Secretary and Treasurer. The company does a business of tanning harness leather, and manufacture horse collars and fly-nets. Their main building is 93x112, built of frame, and mainly four stories high. It was built in 1882 and added to in 1887-89-91. The company employs sixty-five men, with an annual pay-roll of $37,000, and does a business exceeding $130,000 a year.

The T. J. Derwent Company. This company was organized in 1865; incorporated 1890, with a capital stock of $10,000. Its present officers are: T. J. Derwent, President; Thos. Derwent, Vice-President; Luther Derwent, Secretary and Treasurer. They are manufacturers of doors, sash, blinds, stair-work and mouldings, and employ twenty hands, with an annual pay-roll of $12,000; annual product, $50,000. Factory is located south end water power, built of wood, and is 30x100, two stories high.

The Excelsior Dry Plate Company. This firm is located at No. 122 South Second Street. Capital stock, $4,500. Present officers are: P. L. Wright, President; Henry Shedd, Secretary and Treasurer; and produce annually $15,000 worth of their goods. They employ seven hands, with an annual pay-roll of $3,600; factory is of wood, 40x60, two stories high.

FOREST CITY NATIONAL BANK—INTERIOR VIEW.

ROCKFORD PAINT COMPANY.

Dewey's Steam Laundry. W. E. Dewey, proprietor. Capital involved, $2,500. The business amounts to $10,000 per year; employs eight hands, with an annual pay-roll of $3,200. The building is 30x76, one story high.

Eugene Ford. Manufacturer of all kinds of light carriages, and factory located 206 North Wyman Street; amount of capital invested, $4,000, and estimates his annual output at $12,000; gives employment to eight hands, with an annual pay-roll of $5,000. The factory is a frame structure, 44x70 in size, two stories high

Graham's Distillery. This firm consists of Julius, Freeman and Byron Graham, with a capital stock of $150,000. They manufacture sour mash whiskies. The annual product is $300,000. They employ forty-five hands, with an annual pay-roll of $30,000.

A. Hime. Manufacturer of barrels; located 810 Ninth Street. Capital invested, $15,000, and does an annual business of $30,000; gives employment to fifteen hands, with an annual pay-roll of $10,000. The factories are frame, two stories high, 32x50, 24x50, 30x60, and 24x50.

Knapp Shoe Company. This factory is one of Rockford's recent acquisitions, having moved here from Brockton, Mass. They are manufacturers of gents' fine shoes. The capital stock is $75,000. They estimate their annual output at $225,000; will employ 125 hands, with annual pay-roll of $75,000. The factory will be 114x26, three stories high.

T. J. Ryan Packing House. Located on water power. Employ fourteen hands, and do a business of $40,000 per annum, with a pay-roll of $6,000; will build a huge packing house this year on east bank of the river.

The Rockford Shoe Company. This factory is located on North Wyman Street, and are manufacturers of men's fine shoes. The capital stock is $60,000. The present officers are A. C Deming, President; J. W. Irvin, Vice-President; S. C. Tribon, Secretary and Treasurer; company has been organized since August 1880, and do an annual business of $250,000. They give employment to 115 hands, with an annual pay-roll of $50,000. The factory is built of stone and is 53x88, four stories high.

Rockford Paint Manufacturing Company. Is located on Railroad Avenue. The capital stock is $8,000. B. A. Knight is President, and C. Lund, Secretary. They are manufacturers of all kinds of paints, and do a business annually of $12,000; give employment to five hands, with an annual pay-roll of $5,000. The factory is of brick, two stories high, 40x120.

Rockford Oatmeal Company. Manufacturers of oatmeal and Nudavene flakes. Located at corner of Cedar and West Streets. Organized 1882. Rob't H. Tinker, President; Geo. H. Cormack, Vice President and Superintendent; Frank C. King, Secretary and Treasurer. Capital, $120,000. Average annual product, $750,000. Employs eighty hands, with an annual pay-roll of $30,000. Main mill built 1887, of brick, 70x120 feet in size, and four stories high; warehouse, brick, 64x74 feet, four stories high.

Rockford Lubricating Company. Organized July 1889, with a capital of $10,000. John Spafford, President; Miss Anna L. Hull, Secretary and Treasurer. Estimated output, $30,000; manufacture axle grease, lubricating and coach grease; employ six hands, with a pay-roll of $4,860 annually; size of factory, 42x100 feet, two floors.

Rockford Dry Plate Company. Located at 319 W. State street. Capital stock, $3,000. B. F. Greene, Manager; do an annual business amounting to $15,000; employ eight hands, with an annual pay-roll of $3,000.

Rockford Construction Company. This is a Rockford co-partnership, composed of Jones. Woodruff & Co., W. C. Butterworth. Watson Pierpont, D. E. Mead, A. W. Rutledge, and others. They are general contractors in the line of bridge building, paving, water works, construction and also operate brick yards at Rock Island. The business was established in 1888, and the firm employ from one hundred to one thousand hands. Their operations in 1890 exceeded half a million dollars.

The Rockford Baking Company. Located Race Street, water power. was organized December 10, 1889, with a capital stock of $25,000; manufacture crackers and cookies of all kinds. J. W. Bartlett, President; D. G. Spaulding. Vice-President; C. E. Eskelsen, Secretary and Treasurer. Annual product. $60,000; employ thirty hands; pay-roll per year. $12,000. Factory, frame building, 40x75, three stories high.

H. H. Palmer & Company. Manufacturers of churns, creameries, cooperage and general dairy articles. Located at corner of Cedar and Winnebago Streets. Business established in 1879. Capital invested. $50,000; employ about seventy hands, with an annual pay-roll of $27,000 The average annual product is $75,000. Main factory building is of wood, 75x132 feet in size, and two stories high, with warehouse 34x73, on opposite side of the street.

Marsh Mitre Machine. H. C. Marsh, manufacturer. This machine is a mitre and picture frame vise combined. Annual output. $20,000; employs fifteen hands, with a pay-roll of $8,000.

John McDermaid. Manufacturer of the Boss and Star Churns, also dog powers. Factory located at 212 to 220 North Madison Street. Capital invested, $40,000. Annual output, $40,000; employs thirty hands, with an annual pay-roll amounting to $12,000; business established in 1871; factory of wood, 33x66, 36x66, 22x66, two stories high and 33x66, four stories high.

Lovell's Steam Laundry. Located on North Wyman Street. Capital invested, $20,000; do an annual business of $16,000, and give employment to fifteen hands, with an annual pay-roll of $5,000; two-story building, 40x150.

Kauffman Bros. Cigar makers; located at 120 South Main Street, and have been established since 1885. They employ six hands, with an annual output of $16 000. Their annual pay-roll is $3,500; capital invested, $5,000.

Larson & Lundstrom. This firm started a planing mill in October. 1889, in a one-story building, 40x75, on South Wyman Street, on the water power. They turn out mouldings, scroll work, and other house ornamentation, and are doing a business of $12,000, with an annual pay-roll of $4,000. They will employ about ten hands, with an invested capital of $3,000.

Rockford Snuff and Tobacco Company. Is located on Woodruff Avenue. Capital invested, $2,000. Its officers are: Chas. J. Nelson, President; Chas. J. Jones, Secretary; C. J. Anderson, Superintendent. They manufacture all kinds of snuff, and do an annual business of $5,000, and employ two hands, with an annual pay-roll of $1,500. The factory is of brick, two stories high, 31x30.

ROCKFORD CHAIR AND FURNITURE COMPANY.

CLIMAX SLIDE AND CENTER TABLE COMPANY.

Rockford Silver Plate Company. This company is located corner of Elm and Wyman Streets. The capital stock is $125,000; surplus, $50,000. The officers are: H. W. Price, President; A. D. Forbes, Vice-President; G. B. Kelley, Secretary and Treasurer; A. C. Kelley, Assistant Secretary. The company was organized in 1882, coming from Racine, Wis. They manufacture all kinds of silver plate goods, and do a business annually of $225,000. They employ 140 hands with an annual pay-roll of $60,000. The factory is of brick, 90x175, four stories high.

The Rockford Specialty Manufacturing Company. Located at 418 Cedar Street. They manufacture a line of jacket oil-cans, flour sifters, and flour casks G. W. Lane, sole proprietor. He does an annual business of $10,000, and employs seven hands, with an annual pay-roll of $2,800. The factory is of brick, 45x60, two stories high.

Rockford Watch Company. This is perhaps the city's largest industrial concern, and was incorporated in 1874. The present directors are: Henry W. Price, President; William Lathrop, Vice-President; G. E. Knight, Secretary and Treasurer; Levi Rhoades, Israel Sovereign, H. B. Utter, W. H. McCutchan, Peter Sames, J. S. Ticknor, and Irvin French. The capital stock is $282,200, and the company has also a cash surplus of $80,000. They manufacture a complete line of the celebrated Rockford watch movements, and have an average of 300 operatives. Their annual product will foot up to $600,000, and their pay-roll aggregates nearly $250,000. The buildings the company occupies were built in 1875-76, and are located on South Madison Street, on the East Side. They include one four stories high, 40x75 feet in size, another is 40x61, three stories and basement. There is also a large engine and boiler room, and other buildings; all of which are handsomely and substantially constructed of brick and stone.

Rockford Watch Case Company. Located at 112-116 South Main street. Manufacture and repair watch cases, etc. The company was organized in 1872, and has a paid up capital of $70,000. Mr. J. S. Ticknor is President. John Barnes, Vice-President; and A. K. Ticknor, Secretary and Treasurer. The company occupies half of a two story stone and brick building, 66x150 feet in size and with boiler house in rear. The company averages sixty employes, with a pay-roll of $2,000 a month, and an annual product of $50,000.

Peter Sames. Located at corner of Cedar and Church Streets; manufactures wagons of all kinds. Business established in 1858, with an invested capital of $25,000. Present factory built in 1870, is of wood and brick, covering a total area of 110x163 feet, one, two and three stories high; employs about twenty-five hands, with an annual product of $30,000. The annual pay-roll aggregates $12,000.

Searle Sons & Company. Co-partnership, consisting of R. P. Searle, Ed. Searle, and C. E. Bennett, successors to Searle-Bishop Lubricating Co., located 222 North Madison street; capital invested, $10,000; organized November 1890; manufacture "Monarch" Axle Grease and Lubricating Oils; annual product, $20,000; employ six hands, with annual pay-roll of $3,200. Factory of wood, 36x100, two stories high.

Z. B. Sturtevant. Proprietor of the Rockford Flour Mills, located on Mill street on the water power. Capital invested, $75,000; manufactures wheat and rye flour and feed. Employs ten hands, with an annual pay-roll of $7,000. Annual product, $90,000. Mill is built of stone, 40x60 feet in size and four stories high; warehouse adjoining.

ROCKFORD MANTEL AND FURNITURE COMPANY—1890.

The Star Steam Laundry Hamley & Hazard proprietors. Capital invested, $2,500. The business amounts to $8,000 per year; employs seven hands, with an annual pay-roll of $2,700. The building is one story and basement.

Superior Brick Co. This company is located just north of the city limits; its capital stock is $20,000; with E. H. Keeler, President; W. C. Butterworth, Vice-President; H. A. Block, Secretary and Treasurer. They do a business annually of $25,000, and employ fifteen hands, with an annual pay-roll of $10,000.

Skandia Brick Company. Capital stock, $15,000. Gust. Flodell, President; C. J. Jones, Secretary and Treasurer. Manufactures red brick, and with annual product, $30,000. Employ an average of fifty-five hands, with a pay-roll of $15,000.

Swiss Steam Laundry. This firm consists of S. S. Brambaugh and Robt. H. Corse. The business is located at 119 North Main street. They do an annual business amounting to $9,000, and give employment to eleven hands, with an annual pay-roll amounting to $2,500. The size of laundry is 22x107, one story high.

Douglas Ulricl. Book binder. Capital invested, $3,000. Annual out-put. $10,000; employs seven hands, with annual pay-roll of $3,000.

Chas. J. Weldon. Located at 301 and 303 South Main street, and manufactures all kinds of carriages and wagons. Capital invested, $5,000. Employs twelve hands, with an annual pay-roll of $5,000, and does an annual business amounting to $30,000. Factory is a three story frame building, 40x40, with a blacksmith shop 22x40.

L. M. West Manufacturing Company. They are manufacturers of carriage top dressing and harness soaps. Capital stock $40,000. The officers are, L. M. West, President; E. S. West, Vice-President; H. H. West, Secretary. They employ ten hands with an annual pay-roll of $5,000, and do a large business.

Skandia Shoe Manufacturing Company. Is located corner of Fifth street and Seventh avenue; was organized July, 1889, with a capital stock of $50,000. Its present officers are, Aug. P. Floberg, President; G. W. Swanson, Vice-President. N. P. Nelson, Secretary and Treasurer. They manufacture men's and boys' fine shoes, and give employment to fifty hands, with an annual pay roll of $25,000. The annual product is $80,000. The factory is built of brick, 40x100, four stories high with engine room 40x30.

SEMI-MUNICIPAL INSTITUTIONS.

Rockford City Railway Company. Reorganized in 1890. Capital, $150,000; R. N. Baylies, President; G. W. Carse, Secretary. Operate twelve miles of electric railway, with sixteen cars. Employ fifty hands, with an annual pay-roll of $25,000.

West End Street Railway Company. Organized 1890. Capital, $30,000. J. S. Ticknor, President; A. K. Ticknor, Secretary. Operate four miles of electric railway, with six cars; employ twelve men, with an annual pay-roll of $5,000.

Central Union Telephone Company. R. H. Gibbony, Manager. Have 500 local subscribers, and employ twelve hands. Pay-roll $4,500.

ROCKFORD HIGH SCHOOL.

GERMANIA HALL.

Rockford Electric Power Company. Organized 1889. Capital, $70,000. J. W. Bartlett, President; A. L. Bartlett, Secretary. Furnish light and power; occupy three stone buildings on Race Street; employ five hands; annual pay-roll, $2,800.

Forest City Electric Light and Power Company. Organized 1883. Capital, $80,000. E. L. Woodruff, President; M. A. Beal, Secretary. Located on water power. Furnish light and power; employ eighteen men, with an annual pay-roll of $7,200.

American Gas Company. This corporation controls the gas works in a dozen different cities, and secured the Rockford plant in the spring of 1890. It is capitalized at $300,000. The officers are George G. Ramsdell, Vincennes, Ind., President; C. V. Grant, Philadelphia, Secretary; H. S. Whipple, local manager; John M. Kennedy, superintendent. The company manufacture 35,000,000 feet of gas per annum, which is sold at $1.40 to $1.80 per thousand. Last year the company expended $69,000 in laying new mains. They have a total of forty-five miles of mains and supply 550 street lamps. They employ an average of twenty-five men at the works. The value of the gas manufactured is $60,000 per annum, and the pay-roll last year reached $25,000. The gas works was in the hands of the Butterworth family for more than thirty years prior to its acquirement by the present company.

The Rockford Press.

ROCKFORD'S energetic and metropolitan press has been a leading agent in presenting the story of her marvelous growth and in bringing capital and labor within her limits. There are no newspapers in the state, outside of Chicago, that manifest more enterprise or present a more attractive appearance than do the papers of the Forest City. They are all clean cut, bright and ably edited, presenting not only the news of the vicinity but the doings of the world as well. There are four English dailies, a Swedish weekly, a German weekly and temperance and religious weeklies as well. There is also the usual complement of social and education publications and two excellent trade journals.

THE REGISTER-GAZETTE is a coalition of the two pioneer newspapers, and is issued every afternoon. They publish six bright pages, and the editorial columns are devoted to the welfare of the republican cause. Mr. Edgar E. Bartlett is the Secretary of the company and the business head. Mr. W. L. Eaton is the President and Managing Editor. Mr. F. M. Botsford conducts the city department and has Messrs. Alex. McCleneghan and F. E. Sterling on his staff. The daily and weekly issues enjoy a large circulation throughout northern Illinois.

THE MORNING STAR is as bright as its name indicates. It is found at the breakfast table every morning but Monday, and is a handsome eight page paper. It is democratic in politics and the editorial chair is ably held down by Mr. J. Stanley Browne. The business department is controlled by Harry M. Johnson. The city department is looked after by Ralph B. Johnson and Messrs. Frank Edmison, R. C. Chapman and W. C. Johnson are also on the staff.

THE ROCKFORD REPUBLICAN is a newcomer in the field and a lively one. They have two issues each day—morning and afternoon. Each is a large folio in form. The managing editor is Mr. Howard O. Hilton. The business affairs are looked after by Mr. Will J. Johnson. C. D. Allyn is city editor of the evening issue, and

Frank Moran of the morning. The staff also includes Frank Sapp, late of Ottawa Ill.

THE POSTEN is a lively and well-conducted Swedish weekly published and edited by Mr. C. Ebbisen, with J. A. Alden as business manager.

THE GERMANIA is a German publication, issued once a week. John Pingel is publisher, and Rev. Prof. G. J. Kammacher is editor.

TRADE JOURNALS, largely devoted to the furniture interests are also issued by A. F. Judd & Co., and the Forest City Publishing Company. There are numerous religious and class publications issued besides those names, so that it may be seen that the education of the community through the medium of the press is well attended to, and there is "no one thing lacking."

PRINTING AND PUBLISHING.

The Republican Company. (Rep.) Morning and Evening edition Capital, $10,000; H. H. Robinson, President; Will J. Johnson, Secretary: H. O. Hilton, Managing Editor. Organized April 1890. Employs twenty-seven hands, with an annual pay-roll of $18,000. R. S. Morgan has charge of the job department.

Register-Gazette Company. (Rep.) Evening edition. Capital, $36,000. Wm. L. Eaton, President; Edgar E. Bartlett, Secretary and Treasurer. Consolidated Feb. 1, 1891. Employs twenty-three hands, with an annual pay-roll of $18,000.

Rockford Star Printing Company. (Dem.) Morning edition. Capital. $10,000. John D. Waterman, President; H. M. Johnson, Secretary and Treasurer; J. Stanley Browne, Managing Editor. Organized since March 29, 1888. Employs twenty-five hands; annual pay-roll, $15,000.

The Rockford Publishing Company. Publishers and Jobbers of Books and Agents' Novelties; located at 423 East State Street; organized in 1885, with a capital stock of $15,000; Wm. A. Giffen, President; Jas. H. Giffen, Secretary and Treasurer. They employ one hundred people; annual pay-roll $52,500; amount of business done in 1890, $125,000.

The Posten. (Swedish.) Weekly edition. L. M. Noling, President; J. A. Alden, Secretary; C. Ebbisen, Editor-in-chief; employs ten hands, with an annual pay-roll of $3,000.

Chandler Bros. Dealers in books. Do an annual business of $100,000. Employ fifty hands, with an annual pay-roll of $35,000.

F. A. Freeman. Engraver on wood. This gentleman is located over 302 West State street, and has a capital of $2,500 invested in his business, and estimates his annual out put at $5,000; gives employment to four hands, with an annual pay roll of $3,600.

Rockford Engraving Company. Capital invested. $1,000. Do an annual business of $6,000; employs five hands; amount of pay-roll,$4,000.

A. F. Judd & Company. Job printing, 115 and 117 North Madison. Capital, $10,000. A. F. Judd and G. W. Sherer constitute the firm. Do an annual business of $12,000; employ ten hands; annual pay-roll, $5,000.

Forest City Publishing Company. Printing and book bindery. 124 West State street. Established 1866, incorporated 1891; capital. $20,000. Abraham E. Smith, President and Manager; A. Philip Smith, Vice-President; H. J. Eaton, Secretary. Employs fifty five hands, with annual pay-roll $20,000. Theo. W. Clark has charge of the job room and Alex. Moncrieff foreman of press room.

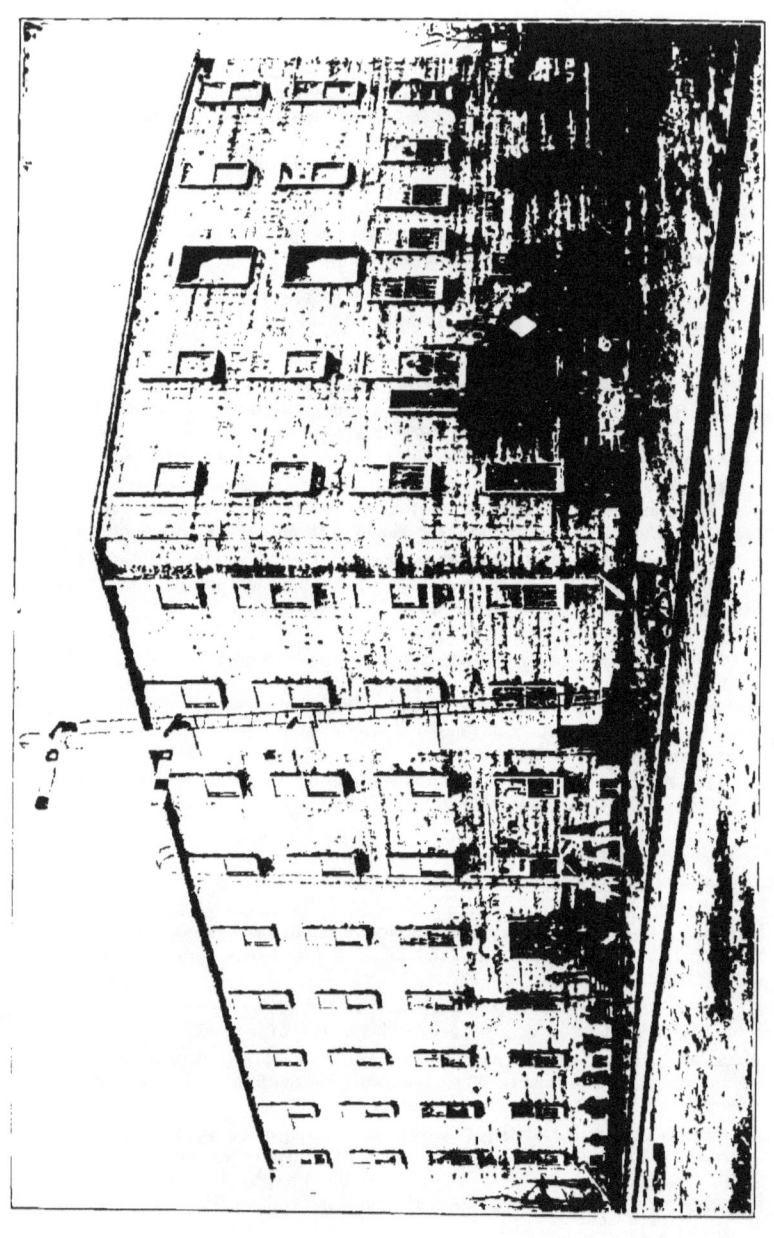

MECHANICS' FURNITURE COMPANY—1890.

UR fair city of Rockford is famous the round world over for her diversified manufactures, and hence no depression in trades can shake her from her foundation. Although furniture is her leading product every factory engaged in its manufacture might close its doors, and still the city could go ahead with progressive strides, and the whistles of her hundreds of other industrial enterprises sound with the same clearness as before. Wood, iron, steel. leather, wool, paper, and every other conceivable material pours into the city day by day to contribute to the mighty aggregate of finished goods that go forth to every land on the habitable globe.

Some idea of the extent of these manufactures may be formed from the following partial list of articles manufactured in the city of Rockford:

Axe handles,	Feed grinders,	Road carts,
Artificial stone,	Gate hinges,	Rocking chairs.
Air brushes,	Gloves,	Regulators.
Ale,	Glucose,	Reversible broilers.
Agricult'l implem'ts,	Gas,	Refrigerators.
Axle grease.	Gavanized iron,	Road scrapers,
Bedsteads,	Glue,	Rubber stamps.
Building paper,	Grain drills,	Rye flour,
Brass goods.	Gas stoves.	Shoes.
Boxes,	Gasoline stoves.	Seeders.
Brick,	Graham flour,	Socks,
Blinds,	Ginger ale,	Stockings.
Bag-holders,	Harrows,	Sleighs.
Bustles.	Harness,	Springs.
Bits,	Hosiery,	Shafting.
Bicycles,	Hand carts.	Steam boilers.
Bed springs,	Horse shoes,	Strainers.
Bath tubs,	Hanging baskets.	Steam fittings,
Bells,	Hat racks.	Steam pumps,
Brooms,	Heaters.	Shirts.
Broom holders,	Hose nozzles,	Sacks.
Boilers,	Harness oil,	Sugar.
Boots.	Hose reel,	Syrup.
Baker's eye-salve,	Hitching posts.	String.
Baking powder,	Horse powers,	Suspenders.
Bags,	Hay presses.	Stair railings.
Bank fixtures,	Hay tedders,	Steam heaters.
Beach curling fluid,	Hangers.	Sash.
Butter color,	Horse muzzles.	Shirt boards,
Barrels,	Harvesters,	Screen doors,
Blank books,	Harness soap,	Silver-plated ware.

ROCKFORD DESK AND FURNITURE COMPANY—1891.

Binders,
Bolts,
Barbed wire.
Beer,
Bedroom suites,
Band saws,
Brackets,
Book-cases,
Boats,
Brushes,
Brass pumps,
Buckwheat flour,
Bread,
Bread toasters,
Bureaus,
Carriages,
Coffins,
Cultivators,
Cotton batting,
Cotton yarn,
Carpets,
Clothes reels,
Cabinets,
Cigars,
Cider,
Confectionery,
Clothing,
Check rowers,
Corn planters,
Corn meal,
Churns,
Crackers,
Cement,
Chemicals,
Chiffoniers,
Carpet stretchers,
Casks,
Cheese,
Chairs,
Canned goods,
Cake,
Corn shellers,
Clocks,
Cough drops,
Coulters,
Circular saws,
Cuffs,

Hose supporters,
Ink,
Iron pumps.
Ironing tables,
Ironware.
Ironworking machn'y,
Iron cutters,
Ice cream,
Jig saws,
Japaned ware,
Jointed hanging hooks,
Jellies,
Jewelry,
Knives,
Knitting machinery,
Knit underwear,
Knit jackets,
Leather,
Lounges,
Lath fencing,
Leather dashers,
Lathes,
Locks,
Log screws,
Lime,
Lawn settees,
Liquid stove polish,
Lard oil
Lamp posts,
Leggings.
Lemon squeezers,
Ladies' underwear,
Lubricating oil,
Leather axle washers,
Mowers,
Mattresses,
Mantels,
Mouse traps,
Malleable iron,
Machine oil,
Monuments,
Mouldings,
Mop handles,
Mill supplies.
Milling machines,
Nails,
Nuts,

Snuff,
Stove-pipe,
Soap,
Side boards,
Steam cocks,
Spring hinges,
Screws,
Scissors,
Sprinklers,
Shawls,
Swill carriers,
Straw board,
Spring beds,
Stamps,
Shoe blacking,
Stove polish,
Sewer pipe,
Step-ladders,
Secretaries,
Surgical instruments,
Slippers,
Saddles,
Sieves.
Snow shovels,
Silverware,
Stall guards,
Sewing machines,
Sorghum machinery,
Silver polish,
Stoves,
Steam engines,
Toilet soaps.
Tacks,
Tank heaters,
Tinware,
Teeth,
Trunks.
Tables,
Teapot stands,
Time locks,
Tire shrinkers.
Tiling,
Toys,
Tools,
Twines,
Tubular well pumps.
Umbrella-holders,

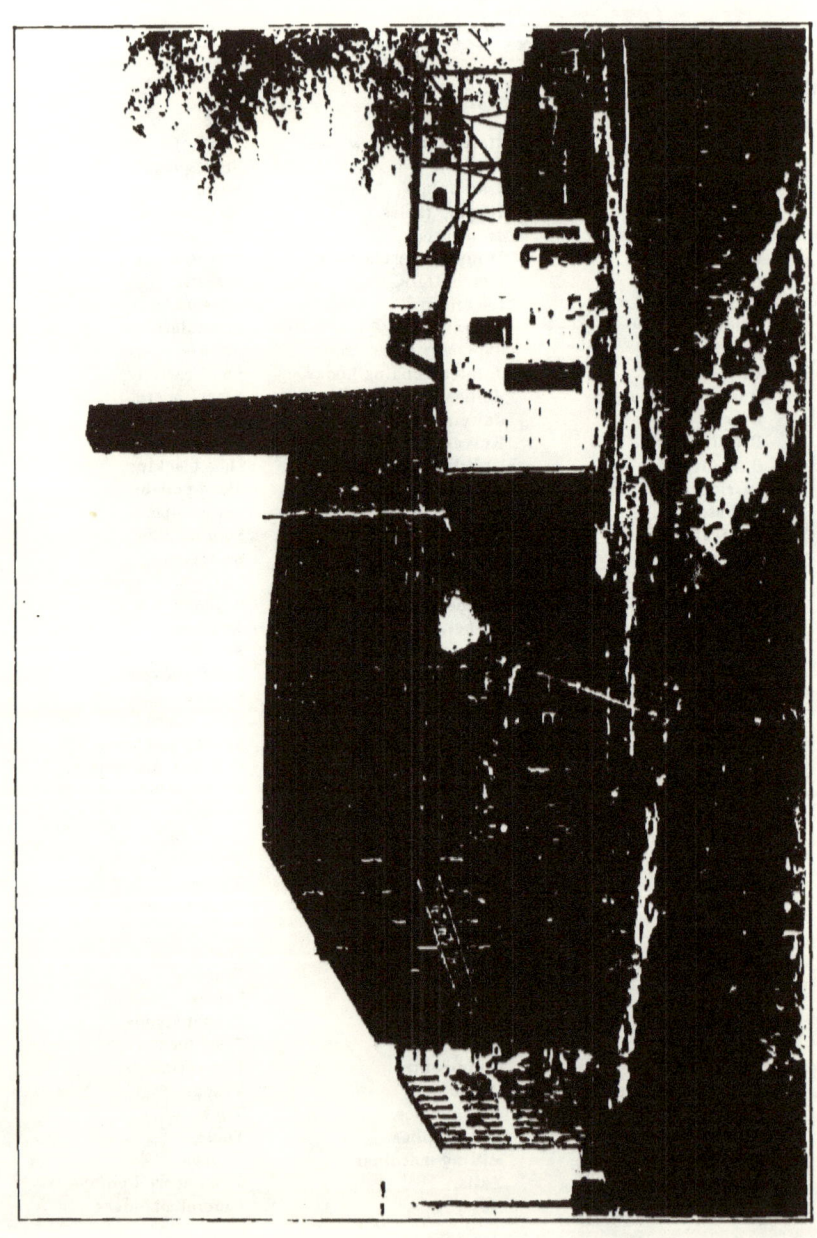

Collars,
Castings,
Concrete walks,
Carriage top dressing.
Drills,
Desks,
Dry plates,
Devore's indest'bl awl.
Door frames,
Derricks,
Dog powers,
Dyes,
Dressed lumber,
Dynamos,
Electric motors.
Electric appliances.
Elevators,
Extracts,
Eggbeaters,
Excelsior,
Egg beaters,
Furniture,
Folding beds,
Flour,
Forks,
Foot power,
Feed,
Fertilizers,
Fanning mills,
Flour sifters,
Flannels,
Feed mills,
Fly nets,
Fire clay,
Flower stands.
Foot rests,
Force pumps,
Feed cookers,
Files,
Fly paper,
Fur garments,

Neckyokes.
Nickel plated ware
Nudavene flakes
Newspapers,
Nickel polish.
Oat meal,
Oil cans,
Oil burners.
Office fixtures,
Overalls,
Organs,
Plows,
Planters.
Paint.
Post hole diggers,
Picture frames,
Pipe holders,
Pasteboard boxes,
Pumping jacks,
Pump cylinders,
Pumps,
Pencil sharpeners,
Pulleys,
Patterns.
Parlor suites,
Potato mashers,
Perfumery,
Pedestals,
Patent medicines,
Pillowsham holders,
Pop,
Prison guards,
Paper,
Punches,
Potato diggers,
Paper holders,
Pocket matches,
Reapers,
Rakes,
Razors,
Stencils,

Universal syphon,
Upholstered goods,
Valises.
Valves,
Vinegar,
Vitrified bricks,
Varnishes,
Watches,
Watch cases,
Watch keys,
Wagons,
Wind mills.
Water wheels,
Warp.
Wheel-barrows,
Washing machines.
Wringers,
Wash-stands,
Whisky,
Well drills,
Wire fencing,
Wire cloth,
Wire signs.
Wire nails,
Wire novelties.
Wrapping paper,
Wrought iron ware,
Woolen goods,
Water casks,
Wood worki'g mach'y,
Willow ware,
Wooden ware,
Wind engines,
Water pipe,
Water tanks,
Wash tubs,
Woolen yarn,
Wood jacket cans.
Wood filler,
Wood cuts.

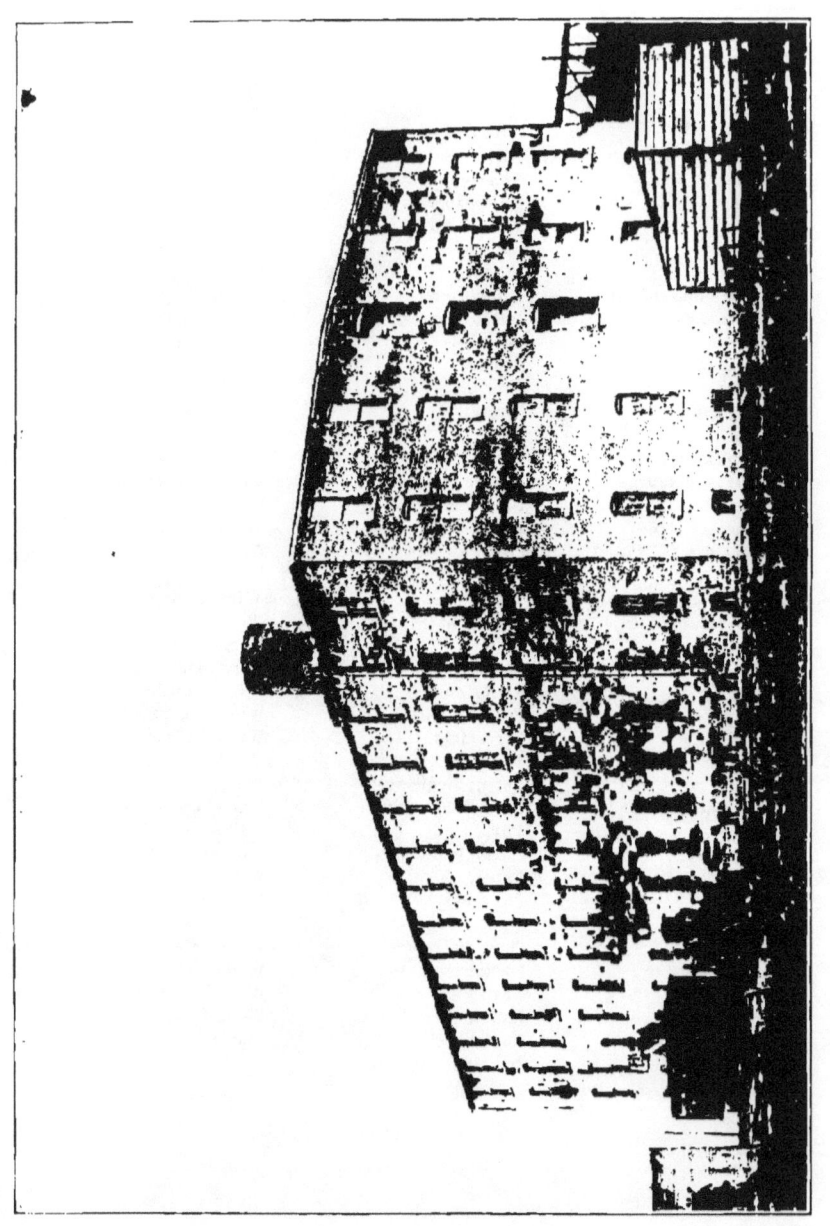

STAR FURNITURE COMPANY—1890.

As a Business Center.

A CITY situated as Rockford is has many advantages as a commercial center. Of course we are too close to Chicago to be a large jobbing center, but on the other hand our proximity to the metropolis of the west gives us low freight rates and good connections with the entire country. We have a number of jobbing houses doing a good business, and more are contemplated. But it is as a manufacturing center on which Rockford's fame mainly rests.

If, however, not a factory had ever been started in the city, still the Forest City would have been a thriving place, merely as a country trading point. In the center of a county of the richest farming lands in the world; whose farms are owned by a prosperous people; mostly clear of mortgages, well stocked, with neat and even elegant houses and spacious barns; a county which never knew a cyclone, a hurricane, or a blight, and seldom a drought, the farming trade enjoyed by our retail merchants is simply enormous. The growth of the city to its present size where it overshadows all cities within a long distance around, enables the merchants to carry immense stocks, and draws trade from a large radius. The retail trade of Rockford, both city and country, would surprise eastern cities of five times its size. There are between five and six hundred retail stores in the city, including some mammoth concerns, using entire three and four story blocks, and including as well a great many smaller establishments. It speaks volumes for their prosperity to say that there has been but three failures in the city during the past year, and the aggregate amount involved in all three was less than $7,000.

The city has eight banks, six of which are national, one state and one private. The banking business has reached such proportions that a clearing house must soon be established. The business men have a Business Men's Association and a Commercial Club, and there will be a Board of Trade established presently.

As a commercial center Rockford is right in line, and within the next two or three years will push forward as she never has before.

Temperance Headquarters.

A MONG the many things which are worthy of especial notice is our local Woman's Christian Temperance Union, who are the happy possessors of a very fine building, which is centrally located at the west end of the city bridge. A lunch and coffee room is conducted by the ladies, which is in charge of a competent matron. The organization is a national one. The local organization is a most excellent one, and is accomplishing very praiseworthy results. The officers are: President, Mrs. T. G. Backus; Vice-President-at-large, Mrs. Rev. W. A. Phillips; Recording Secretary, Mrs. Margaret Skiff; Corresponding Secretary, Mrs. P. R. Wood; Treasurer, Miss Julia L. Worthington. Regular meetings are held every Thursday afternoon and on Sunday at 3 o'clock.

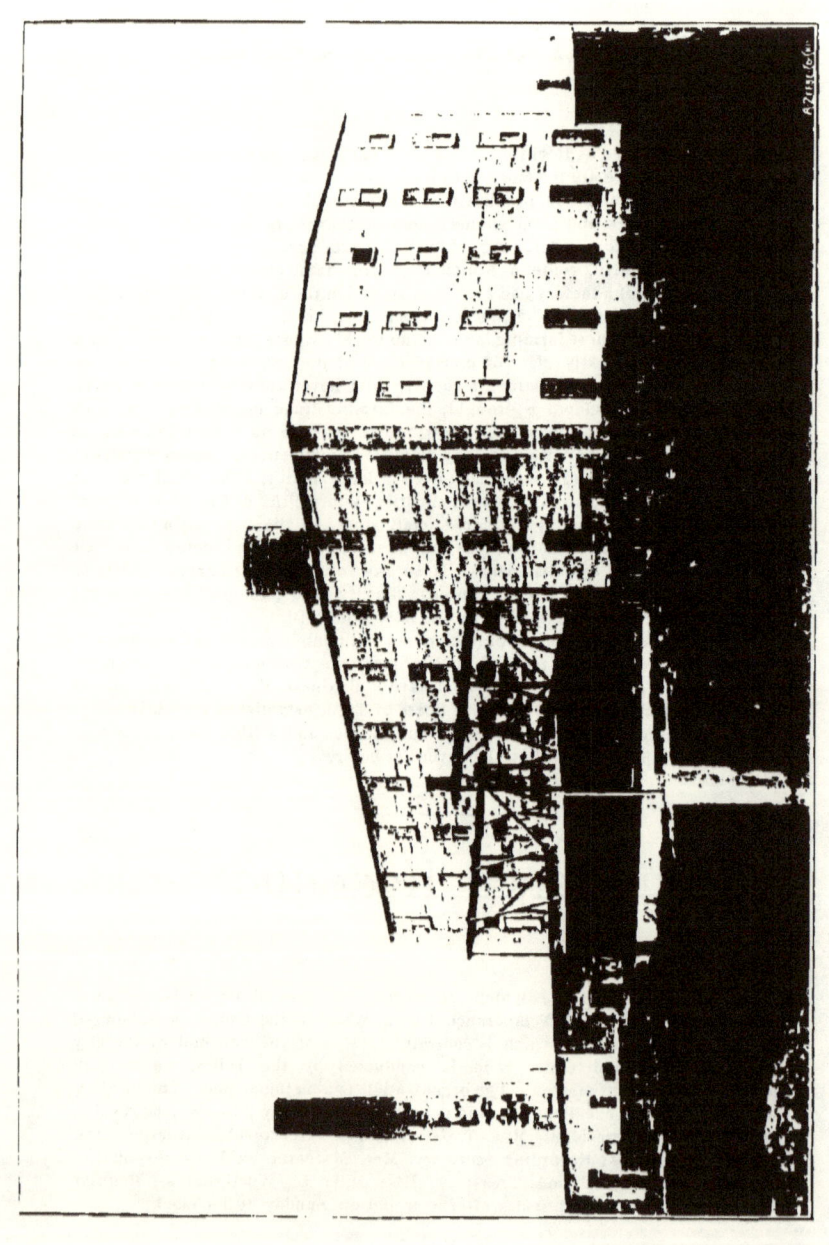

WEST END FURNITURE FACTORY—1891

Our Thespian Temple.

LOVERS of dramatic and operatic amusements are well cared for in the Forest City. The Rockford Opera House is a large, handsome brick structure, on North Wyman Street, costing, with recent improvements, $50,000, and is elegantly fitted up and well supplied with all modern convenience, scenery and stage settings. Its seating capacity is fifteen hundred. The management is fully awake to the needs of the public, and presents the amusement-loving people with a spendid list of attractions, such as the Daly, Madison Square, and Lyceum companies; Modjeska, Janauschek, Booth, Kean, Nat Goodwin, Sol Smith Russell, and Bostonians. The house is under the personal management of C. C. Jones, who is assisted by Maurice B. Field.

The City Hospital.

NO institution in the city covers a wider field of usefulness; none does so much to alleviate human suffering; nor so much real, necessary and unostentatious good, as the Rockford City Hospital. It is under the ownership and control of the Rockford Hospital Association, which consists of 262 individuals who contributed toward the establishment of the institution. This association was organized in the year 1883, and was due largely to the efforts of W. A. Talcott, Dr. W. H. Fitch, and a number of other people who had become cognizant of the great need of a place to care for the victims of accidents, the sick and afflicted. The matter was agitated during the year, and in December the agitation crystalized into action. The association was formed and incorporated. A valuable piece of property centrally located on the corner of South Court and Chestnut Streets was purchased. There was a large brick house on the lot and this was fitted up for use, nearly everything necessary being donated. Judge Wm. Brown was elected as President of the association and Mrs. S. B. Wilkins, Vice President, for the first year, and Wm. A. Talcott was made Secretary and Treasurer, which position he has since held.

Mrs. M. J. Smith was selected for matron, and still holds that important post. It was an exceedingly wise choice. "Aunt Jane," as she is known all over the city, is a born nurse, and under her administration the utmost good has been accomplished with the means at hand.

In 1887 efforts began to be made for a larger building, especially for the use of the hospital. This was erected during the winter and dedicated in March, 1888. It is a splendid three-story brick edifice, facing on Chestnut Street, costing $15,000. It accommodates thirty patients and is supplied with every convenience. The old hospital building stands just east of it, is connected by a hall and is used by the matron and nurses as living rooms.

Shortly after it was erected, Horatio Stone, who has ever been an enthusiastic supporter of the institution, and who is now president of the association, donated an elevator costing $1,500. A new operating room has just been completed on the west side of the main building, the old one having been found to be too small. This new

PHŒNIX FURNITURE COMPANY—1891.

addition is built by Mrs. Ralph Emerson in memory of her son, Ralph Emerson, Jr.

The hospital is always as full as the management will allow. Daily, almost, the patrol wagon brings some poor fellow, mangled by an accident, to the door. Besides this, cases of sickness are cared for as soon as possible. When the patients are able, they are expected to pay, but when they cannot, they receive the same care.

Necessarily, running an institution on such a plan, it cannot be nearly self-supporting, and the hospital depends upon voluntary subscriptions and annual collections which are taken up in the various city churches. Funds are constantly lacking to do the work required. If some one would leave a bequest in such a way that a regular income could be assured, the effectiveness of the hospital would be greatly increased.

The present officers of the association are: Horatio Stone, President; Mrs. Jane G. Wilkins, Vice-President; W. A. Talcott, Secretary and Treasurer.

The Public Library.

AS an important element in giving to the city its old world aroma of culture its public library is entitled to important consideration. Books, if well chosen, are the best and most considerate of companions, and the records of the library indicate that in Rockford the creations of master minds go alike into mansion and cottage. The library was first opened in 1873, and has grown to extensive proportions. There are now twenty thousand well-chosen volumes on its shelves and new books are added almost as fast as they come from the press. The library occupies commodious quarters over the postoffice, and a large public reading room, supplied with the leading newspapers and magazines, is a valuable auxiliary. That these advantages are offered to the public evenings and Sundays is an evidence of the liberal educational spirit of the hour. The number of those entitled to draw books from the library is over ten thousand. Mr. W. Rowland is the efficient librarian in charge; Miss Lizzie Williamson, assistant.

Social Pleasures and Society.

PROBABLY many of our friends in the eastern states feel somewhat surprised at the many social advantages that may be enjoyed throughout this section of the country, but nowhere are these social features in any degree superior to those at Rockford. While the busy hum of machinery is heard on every side of the "gem of Illinois," yet human desire for friendly comminglings is as apparent here as in the most fashionable of eastern cities, and amid the noise and bustle of a booming city the efforts to drive off dull care for a short season are as assiduously pursued as the most fastidious might desire. Every church congregation has its social and literary circle, and the secret and benevolent societies have their regular "blow outs." Then there are a great many social clubs of various kinds, which hold meetings weekly, and there are progressive cinch and euchre clubs, married people's, card clubs, and all kinds of clubs organized by various cliques for informal amusements.

UNION FURNITURE COMPANY.

Rockford Y. M. C. A.

ⓞNE of the finest buildings of its kind in the country, is the Young Men's Christian Association, located at the corner of North Madison and East State streets. The edifice is a very handsome one costing $50,000, and is a monument of the generous and practical interest of nearly eight hundred contributors; persons who believe in and desire to perpetuate this noble institution, which has for its object the spiritual, intellectual upbuilding and uplifting of young men. Meetings are held at various times during the week, and Sunday afternoon from 4 to 5 o'clock, Young Men's Gospel Meetings are held, which are largely attended. The gymnasium is fully equipped with bars, rings, ladders, &c., and is under the personal charge of General Secretary E. M. Aiken. It is a grand good thing, and many a young man finds a helping hand extended to him in his need. The present officers are S. F. Weyburn, President; E. M. Aiken, General Secretary; H. T. Hansen, Assistant Secretary.

A City of Fine Dwellings.

Ⓟ O person visits Rockford without being impressed with the beauty and comfort of her homes. Rockford people are "here to stay" as the expression goes, and they build themselves homes where it is a pleasure to reside, not simply a place to stay for a season. One feature which is especially noteworthy and which strikes visitors from other factory cities as peculiarly strange, is that the people generally, in fact universally, own their own homes. The laborers and factory people, as well as the business men, manufacturers, professional men and capitalists, own their own residences, and very tasty, and convenient ones, too. Thousands of pretty homes, every one of which is the castle of some man, well kept, and surrounded by a hundred evidences of the care which a man devotes to his own, tells a story of prosperity and happiness more eloquent than words can paint.

Rockford has but few grand castles. Few of her homes, even where wealth and magnificence reside, have that exterior of gorgeous splendor which are visible in some places. While there are many fine houses, it is in the grounds surrounding them which are most striking for beauty. Nowhere in the West is there a city where the grounds will compare with those of Rockford. The homes set back among the groves, and well kept lawns are a constant picture to the eye.

Rockford is noted for her numberless fine residences belonging to what is called the middle class; people who do not live on their means, but are engaged in active business. There are hundreds of these, fashioned in novel styles of architecture and not crowded into undue proximity to one another. These homes are really elegant in their architecture and appointments, and give the city a most prosperous and distinguished appearance. Then the houses of the mechanics. It is a constant

EXCELSIOR FURNITURE COMPANY.

wonder to the visitor at Rockford to observe the residences owned and occupied by our mechanics and laboring people. All through the Swedish district particularly, the houses are models of beauty and comfort. They are prettily designed, well built, always two stories high and often two and a half—and what is better, they are owned and generally paid for by the people who occupy them. The grounds are nicely kept and the people take pride in beautifying and improving the looks of the city and of their own places.

Shade trees are abundant, so much so that the city has gained the appellation "The Forest City." The most elegant street is North Main street, which is lined on either side by the houses of Rockford's wealthiest people. On the east side of the street the lots run clear to the river. These river bank lots are very beautiful, and as there are no fences for nearly the entire distance of the fine residence district—over a mile—it has the appearance of an elegant park.

On the East Side East State street is the most elegant thoroughfare. All along up the hill the street is lined with handsome grounds and fine houses. South Third street also contains some very handsome residences.

One distinguishing feature of Rockford houses is that most of them are built of wood. There are comparatively few brick residences. Even where a large amount of money is put into the building, they are built of wood. There are a few notable exceptions, but as a class Rockford houses are built of wood.

The interiors of Rockford houses are even : more pleasing than their exteriors. Comfortably and in many cases elegantly furnished they are really "homes," not simply places to stay. It is Rockford's homes and the home-life of her people which makes the Forest City such a delightful place to live in and draws people so easily to her borders.

Rockford Driving Club.

Ⓣ HE park consists of ninety acres of land in the north end of the city immediately on the line of the C. M. & St. P. railroad, the driving park being situated just west of the track. This park is one of the most thoroughly equipped in the country, containing all the modern improvements for taking care of the trotting stock, there being 150 excellently constructed stalls. The grand stand is a commodious and artistic affair with a seating capacity of 2500, and is provided with comfortable chairs for the accommodation of its patrons. The track is kite shaped. This track has proved a record-breaker, as every animal that has won a race on the track has lowered his record in order to do so. The park is most delightfully situated, commanding the most charming view of nature's diversified beauties, in which no other country on the globe is more prolific than is the country surrounding the city of Rockford, for in every direction one may look new scenes are presented to the vision, which is limited only by the capacity of the eye. The Rockford Driving Club was licensed to organize in 1889. The officers are, Frank G. Smith, President; H. H. Palmer, Vice-President; C. C. Jones, Secretary, and Geo. L. Woodruff, Treasurer. There are two meetings a year, held one in June and the other in August.

The Lowell of the West.

IT has not taken half a century to demonstrate that Rockford is the industrial city of the Mississippi Valley. Two decades ago the vastness of her manufactures gave to her the sobriquet of the "Lowell of the West," and this clings to her still, although it is not worn with as much pride as in other days, for Rockford, mind you, is passing this namesake of hers, and it may soon be that Lowell will feel a dignified desire to be known as the Rockford of the East. The agricultural implement industry was one of the first to seek a home in Rockford and bear her name abroad. Next came the era of furniture factories, and now there is but one city in the land that turns out more furniture than she. There are twenty factories in this line alone. There are cotton, woolen, paper and knitting mills, and they are all spreading out and increasing. Two of the largest watch factories in the country are now located here, and there is also a watch case factory and a huge silver plating concern. From other cities a dozen industries have brought their plants to Rockford, but, better still, her own citizens have put their hands in their purses and furnished the capital for a large majority of her factories, and are to-day profitably operating them. It is more especially within the last two years that the eyes of the outside world were drawn to this manufacturing center. The advent of another trunk line of railroad and the establishment of a number of important industries, created considerable interest, and it was found that here was a city of marvelous growth without any brass band attachment. Manufacturers learned that a town of 150 paying industries, with all the prestige that goes with that statement would open its doors to them: a city possessing all natural and commercial advantages, and some other facilities that no other place could boast of. Since this discovery has become more generally advertised this little metropolis has made marvelous strides. The census report, showing that the per cent. of gain in a decade led almost the entire state, still further added to her fame, until there is not a citizen within her borders, nor a drummer on the road but that claims that Rockford will be the second city in the state within ten years. She is destined to claim at least one hundred thousand inhabitants, and with the diversity of her industries and her independence from tributary agriculture, it is difficult to conceive a combination of circumstances that could give her a black eye. She is a city not alone for to-day but for all time. When the last trumpet shall sound there will be at least one hundred thousand Rockfordites ready to don their crowns and take their places in the celestial choir. The smoke of her factory chimneys paints her story on the sky. It is a tale of energy, industry and progress. She does not "boom"—she quick-steps with the sturdy stride of an army with banners. She welcomes legitimate industry and furnishes liberal aid, but she is careful of her reputation, and wants no unprofitable "snap" concerns looking for a bonus. All the factories that have more recently come within the limits of Rockford have been fully investigated and found profitable. Upon finding the city has opened its purse, subscribed liberally to stock, and donated buildings and sites. This is still her program and pronunciamento. Any further facts regarding the city that may be desired will be cheerfully imparted by the Business Mens' Association, the Real Estate Exchange, the Commercial Club, or the firm or individual from whom this little work came.

RESIDENCE OF H. W. PRICE.

RESIDENCE OF OSCAR NELSON.

Municipal Improvements.

FEW things more clearly indicate the progressive spirit that obtains in Rockford more substantially than does the mention of the municipal operations, which were so cheerfully undertaken and satisfactorily consummated during the year 1890. Two new bridges were built across Rock River, and one moved to another site, making six in all; a dozen bridges were built over Kent's and Keith's Creek, and other bridges were repaired, the whole cost of the operations in this department exceeding $122,000. The street paving included nearly two miles of cedar blocks, and cost upwards of $60,000. Five miles were added to the sewer system at an expense exceeding $40,000. The water mains were extended and a new engine put in, at a cost of $40,000. A handsome school house was erected at an outlay of nearly $25,000. These are but samples of what the municipality is doing for itself, and all with but a trifling fraction added to the general tax levy. This year the sewer system will be extended to a total of twenty miles of mains; two miles of brick pavement and one of cedar block will be laid; the police and fire departments will be enlarged, and many other municipal improvements made, the whole costing at least $200,000, and all with a slight reduction from the general tax of the previous year. The city government has always been clean and business-like. To the administration of Mayor John H. Sherratt and his coadjutors the community owes much, and it is felt that the present mayor and council will retain the mantle of progress which fell upon their shoulders. The municipal management is in the following hands:

MAYOR—HARRY N. STARR.
CITY CLERK—F. G. HOGLAND.
CITY ATTORNEY—R. K. WELSH.
CITY TREASURER—J. D. WATERMAN.
POLICE MAGISTRATE—L. L. MORRISON.
HEALTH OFFICER—DR. W. A. BOYD.
CITY ENGINEER—D. C. DUNLAP.

Aldermen
First Ward—HARRY WOOLSEY, R. A. SHEPHERD.
Second Ward—E. W. BROWN, A. J. ANDERSON.
Third Ward—T. J. DERWENT, Z. B. STURTEVANT.
Fourth Ward—WILLIS M. KIMBALL, L. A. WEYBURN.
Fifth Ward—O. P. TRABERS, W. L. HARBISON.
Sixth Ward—G. A. SALSTROM, W. D. CLARK.
Seventh Ward—THOS. W. COLE, D. G. SPAULDING.

Two Valuable Parks.

OUT beyond the confines of the beautiful Forest City, to the north, and situated on the banks of the placid Rock River, Harlem Park, the new creation of the enterprising spirit which animates all Rockford, offers to the wearied in body and burdened in mind relaxation, recreation and rest. Rich in rustic beauties and general attractions, it affords a pleasant refuge and retreat from the cares of every day life and business, refreshing the physical and

UTTER MANUFACTURING COMPANY'S PLANT.

CENTRAL FURNITURE FACTORY.

mental faculties, and rendering to enervated nature greater and more beneficial aid than potions and lotions from the shelves of pharmacies, or the sparkling waters from the fountain of universal youth.

A new element of restorative power, a tonic to the dispirited, a real and vital izing force to instill life and activity into frames where torpor and languidity reigns, presents itself in the Switchback Railway, a new and popular feature of amusement which is at present attracting the attention and awakening the interest of thousands. Seated in its easy car for a rapid flight over its hills and wondrous vales, one forgets everything but the fact that time, space, and every surrounding object are being annihilated by the rush of its whirring wheels, and remembers that, only when the few seconds sufficing for the journey have passed into infinity. The genius of its inventor has brought joy and pleasure to youth and new experiences to age which will be remembered when the invention has passed into innocuous desuetude.

Other factors for the promotion of pleasure are the band concerts which occur twice a week in the elaborate band stand and pavillion erected for the promotion of the pleasure of the music loving visitors. Twelve arc lights shed their effulgence over the scene on the evenings devoted to the enjoyment of this most elevating art, and render Luna an unnecessary expense to the solar lighting system. Every thing that nature has left undone in the creation of a park of wondrous beauty has been undertaken by mortal hands, and success has crowned every effort to render its attractiveness more attractive. The cool, refreshing shades of the park are meccas much sought by all classes of people. The rich, the poor, the high, the low, all meet on an equal footing beneath its waving foliage and on its emerald carpet. Rank, station, all are forgotten in the fact that nature is the common mother of all, and each and every one seeks pleasure in those sports in which their estimate of real enjoyment finds satisfaction.

Beautiful Harlem Park is but ten minutes ride from the business centers on the electric railway, and is accessible by boat and carriage. A dock gives landing to passengers from the steamers, and a beautiful driveway leads along the shore of the river to the park confines. It is an attraction which lends to the Forest City another grace, and is a fount of exquisite pleasure to the lovers of nature as well as those who seek its limits from more sordid and grosser motives; and a cordial welcome is extended to the visitor by those who have the management of the grounds. With lovely scenery to charm the eye and delight the mind, with melodious harmonies to please the tuneful ear, and its host of amusements to entertain, Harlem Park is destined to become one of the most popular and much frequented resorts within an extended radius. Mr. Chas. Brumbaugh, the genial superintendent, and Mr. John Camlin, the efficient and courteous secretary, are developing new and richer resources of pleasure, and the future will open the door to wider possibilities and the achievement of greater results.

The second park that lies without the city's walls and is still easily accessible, is the West End Recreation Park, used for the grounds of the Rockford league base ball club. The park lies in the famous West End addition, on the line of the new electric railway, whose handsome olive green cars are the cynosure of all eyes. The grounds are neatly fenced and contain a large amphitheatre capable of seating the enthusiastic hundreds of admirers of the national game that the Forest City contains. The park is to be further improved and developed, and near by the lofty tower of the West End observatory will be reared. The whole is within a few minutes ride of the city's heart.

S. B. WILKINS COMPANY KNITTING FACTORY.

ROCKFORD OAT MEAL MILL.

The Hotels of Rockford.

THE Forest City has a number of excellent houses where the traveler may find rest and refreshment, and there are more coming. The New Holland and The Wilson are both operated by Irve Leonard, and are the leading hotels of the town, receiving nearly all the commercial patronage. The Holland is a handsome four-story building, occupying half a square, and contains eighty well-furnished rooms. The Wilson, which was formerly known as The Leonard, has fifty rooms, and is located on West State Street. The Hotel Noonan is a very comfortable and popular house containing twenty-five handsome rooms. The Chick House is located diagonally across from The Holland and has some forty rooms. It is well patronized. The Commercial, American and Forest City Houses are of a cheaper grade.

Within a few weeks from the date of issuance of this book ground will be broken for a magnificent hotel to be located on South Main street, one block South of The Holland. It will have six floors and will cover half a block. It will be called The Nelson, and will contain two hundred rooms. The cost, including furnishing and decoration will be $225,000, and a well-known Chicago hotel man will be lessee.

Plans are also in view for a large hotel and opera house on the East Side, to cost $150,000. The opera house feature will probably materialize at any rate.

Rockford's Future.

IT needs no pen of seer or prophet to cast the horoscope of the Forest City. When a man stands at the threshold of maturity, and is sober, honest, healthy, industrious, careful and rich, it needs no necromancer's art to say what he will be ten or twenty years hence. The world would be grievously disappointed did he not prove healthier, wealthier, and wiser. So with Rockford. A city standing in so promising a position as she fills to-day cannot well help making a lofty record among the municipalities of the world, as the years develop. There is no pent-up Utica in Winnebago County, Illinois. A city set upon a hill cannot be hid. Millions of dollars are invested within her limits every year. All ventures are legitimate. There is no bubble to burst; no boom to prick; no mushroom to grow and shrivel. Her own citizens have unbounded faith in her future. They do not talk of moving away. Few of them invest surplus money in southern pine or Kansas mortgages. They put their good old stuff in Rockford and watch it grow in volume as the months go by. They do not take chances in thus disposing of their funds. Real estate is held comparatively cheap, and every house erected finds a buyer or tenant anxiously awaiting the key. There is an assured profit on every investment in home building, and so local capital remains local capital, instead of seeking some doubtful speculation in western wilds, chimerical corporations or vapor baths. It is needless to deduce Rockford's future from this. It is a known quantity. Come and take a hand in it if you will.

ROCKFORD CITY HOSPITAL.

ROCKFORD CABINET COMPANY.

What Rockford Wants.

I N every work of this character, every city write-up, every boom edition, you will find a chapter or article describing the city's needs. It is different here. Rockford asks not the earthly praise or prayer of any one. She has lots of bridges, railroads, paved streets, city lights, water, gas and street cars, and her citizens have all the pie and ice cream they can eat. Almost everything that is turned out by the manufactories of the land is the product of some one of her hundreds of industries. She is handsomely lodged, well fed and neatly dressed. There is absolutely nothing that she needs to insure her happiness or permanence. And yet, as in every prosperous household, the aroma of hospitality is abroad. She welcomes all good and honorable citizens. The visiting manufacturer finds greeting and co-operation: the statesman, the merchant and the commercial tourist are alike cordially received; even the tramp may stay out of jail so long as he is decently behaved. In fact Rockford welcomes the universe. She may not need you but she can at least find time to take off her working apron and assure you that she is glad you are here. That is the kind of a hair-pin Rockford is.

Young Men to the Front.

T O the average visitor to Rockford an astonishing circumstance is the leadership which the young men have attained. This youthful blood has had much to do with the weal of the municipality, and seems to course with energy through its every vein. The young men are called "the city builders," and there is a coterie of half a hundred of them who have been foremost in nearly all the recent enterprises that have added to the city's wealth and importance. They are tireless workers, but poor boarders, for every dollar of profit gained in one venture is at once embarked in some new enterprise. They take chances, too, but governing it all is that ability for financial forecast that becomes a trait of American character when thrown into active business. It is the young man who is now called higher by his fellows. He fills the mayor's chair, and the council is drawn from his ranks. Even the halls of congress or the governor's mansion are not denied him. In Rockford he rules the roost. Development has been such that beards are no longer necessary to inspire confidence, and one who is on the sunny side of thirty may be president of a bank or corporation, or have manifold interests in his keeping. The young man with the small capital has been heard from. He is adding to his store, and his active business methods inspire the good will of his associates. He is soon at the front. There are men in Rockford who have not yet commenced to think of celebrating their thirty-fifth birthday who are in one way or another connected with all the way from a dozen to twenty different enterprises and find time to carry a knowledge of them all. It is small wonder then that the young man commands so strong a regard in the public mind. Great is the City Builder, and the welfare of Rockford is his "profit."

GRAHAM'S COTTON MILLS.

GRAHAM'S DISTILLERY.

Tale of Two Years.

WITHIN the rolling time of two "great suns" the advance of Rockford has challenged the admiration of the country. Two years have added fifty per cent. to her population, and have started twenty-seven new factories within her borders. A dozen other industries have each doubled their capacity, and others still have greatly increased their business. Nearly one thousand homes have been built, and the character of the city's business blocks has entirely changed. Over $8,000,000 have been invested in manufacturing, building or financial enterprises, and it is apparently but a start. A $225,000 hotel, a $150,000 office building, a $200,000 watch factory, are but examples of ventures to which present efforts are being turned, and there are still greater things in a neophytic condition. The two years just passed have but spurred the community on to greater efforts. The millions of brick that have been laid are but a tithe of those that are to follow. They do not go to build any Chinese wall, however, but to build busy hives of industry and commerce, where honest labor will find a welcome and honest capital a fit remuneration.

The Swedish Citizens.

THE foreign element of the population of the city is mainly composed of the peaceful and industrious sons of Sweden, who make the best citizens that reach this country from other lands. Rockford owes much to them, and the claim that we are the industrial city of the west is made substantial through their efforts. They number one-third the population of the city, and every one is proud of it. The enterprises they control are vast in character, and they are also extensively interested in many ventures conducted by Americans to the manor born. A large insurance company, a mammoth building and loan association, and two substantial banks are financial corporations controlled by them. The largest Swedish church and congregation in the United States is located here, and there are seven other churches where services are conducted in that language. There are 145 Swedish firms or individuals in business, and no failures among them. Their total investments in commercial and financial ventures exceed $8,000,000, and their real estate holdings will reach nearly as much more. They control nearly forty prominent industrial concerns, and it is to them that the community owes the co-operative idea of running factories, which is an effective barrier against strikes and labor troubles. They are a modest, peaceful class of citizens, seldom interfering or aggressive in politics; always industrious and frugal. Their work ingmen own their homes, and they are the finest residences that any class of labor in the country can boast of. They are all two-story dwellings of modern construction, and it is the rule rather than the exception that they cost over $1,500 each. They have built up one of the handsomest manufacturing districts in the world. To the stranger it is a marvel how such things can be, but the native Rockfordite

NELSON KNITTING COMPANY.

GLOBE CLOTHING COMPANY.

no longer feels surprised if his Swedish friend out-does him in home building. They are citizens of whom any community might feel justly proud, and there are a number of leaders among them who are found in the front rank in every enterprise with which the welfare of the city is in anywise connected. Some there are whose names will be found as stockholders or directors in a score of different ventures, and one man at least is an officer in ten corporations. Active men of business they all are and it is one of the brightest jewels in Rockford's crown that so many dwellers within her limits are the fair-haired and pink-cheeked sons and daughters of Svea.

Electricity in Rockford

THIS magnificent force of modern times which puts to shame all the genii of oriental fable has been a prime factor in the city's development. It is chained to various uses. Light, power, motion, in their best forms, own electricity as parent. The city contains an almost unrivalled system of electric street railway. There are two companies who have expended at least $200,000 in providing rapid transit to all parts of Rockford and her thriving suburbs. The Rockford City Railway traverses twenty-six different streets and have fourteen miles of track in service. They have franchises for four miles more which will be laid as soon as possible. They operate twenty cars at present. They reach the principal manufacturing and residence districts and also lead out to Harlem park and the grounds of the Rockford Driving Club. Their service will be enlarged and made perfect ere the season closes.

The West End Street Railway passes through ten streets and avenues and reaches the large factory and residence additions in the west and northwest portions of the city. They also run to the Rockford base ball park and the West End Observatory. They have about six miles of track and are now running six handsome cars, the line starting at the Holland House corner in the heart of the city. The company is also seeking a franchise to penetrate the East Side.

There are two large companies who furnish light and power and their wires extend all over the city and into the additions. The incandescent light is in almost general use in stores and residences, and most of the large factories operate complete plants of their own. There are also a great many arc lights used in stores and for out-door illumination. The city is now formulating a plan whereby it will own its own electric lighting plant and illuminate the streets with almost noon-day splendor.

The telegraph and telephone service also show that this branch of electrical service is most valuable. The offices of the Western Union are open constantly, and their business at Rockford is very great.

The telephone system and service in Rockford is the best in the state. There are five hundred subscribers, which makes the office rank next to Chicago in business. In the central part of the city the lines are run in cables, with one hundred wires in each. This prevents entanglements with the lines of the electric light and railway companies.

The Rockford Electric Manufacturing Company, who turn out dynamos and all manner of electrical appliances, is also a large and thriving institution of this city.

ROCKFORD BOLT WORKS.

ROCKFORD MITTEN AND HOSIERY COMPANY.

Music in the Forest City.

WHILE on every side we see evidences of the rapid and steady growth of our city, and Rockford's industries have won for her merited recognition in every state in the Union, yet not alone to busy manufactories, to successful business enterprises, nor to beauty of location is due the precedence which she has attained. But the energy which has made our industries a success, has at the same time been used for the advancement of our educational institutions, and the cultivation of the fine arts, and these, united, have made Rockford the ideal city of the west. Side by side with our material advancement has been the onward progress of musical culture in our midst.

The conservatory of music in connection with the Seminary is an outgrowth of Prof. D. N. Hood's untiring labor in the capacity of musical instructor in that institution, a position which he has held since 1858. From this conservatory have graduated many young women whose musical talent has attracted more than local notice, and not a few of these now grace Rockford's musical circles and wield an influence in society such as musicians devoted to their art, alone possess.

An outgrowth of the Seminary Conservatory is the Mendelssohn Club, an organization which was formed in October 1884. The original membership numbered forty ladies, of whom nearly all were graduates of the Conservatory of Music and some of whom had continued their studies abroad. Mrs. Chandler Starr has been the president of the Club for seven years and to her enthusiasm is largely due the success of the organization, since by her executive ability and musical attainments she has been both an efficient guide and an inspiration. The meetings are held every two weeks during eight months of the year, one-half of the membership furnishing the program for each meeting. Thus thorough and constant practice is required of the members and a wide range of composers studied, a work of the individual members which probably no musical society in the west has before successfully maintained. In 1888, honorary members were received into this society for the first time and they now number seventy ladies who are admitted to the meetings and annual musicales. However, the efforts of the Mendelssohn Club have not been for their own exclusive improvement, but for their annual complimentary concerts they have brought to our city some of the best musical talent available at the west, and thus given to hundreds of our people the pleasure and the culture which alone can be secured from such a source. Among the artists thus secured were Messrs. Liebling, Becker and Eicheim for a chamber concert in 1886, Mme. Fannie Bloomfield and Signorina Varesi in 1888. Mme. Teresa Carreno, assisted by the Mendelssohn ladies' chorus, in 1889, and in May of this year the Mendelssohn Quintette of Boston. Besides these artists, they also secured Miss Neally Stevens, of Chicago, for piano recital, Miss Amy Fay for piano conversation, and Mr. Frank Fisher Powers and Mrs. Gerritt Smith, vocalists. The society has itself given several concerts which show the good work accomplished by the members, and have won for them a reputation of which we may justly feel proud.

Besides the pianists of the club its membership includes many vocalists of merit, and from their number has sprung the Ladies' Mendelssohn Quartette, which is now readily conceded to have no superior in any western city. Their

RESIDENCE OF H. H. HAMILTON.

RESIDENCE OF MRS. W. D. TRAHERN.

soprano, Miss Addie St. John, is spending several months in England, further cultivating her voice under the guidance of the renowned instructor, Shakespeare.

The Weber Quartette is a company so well known to the cities throughout the West, that it requires no introduction, and needs no words of praise. It consists of Messrs. Myron Barnes, Chas. Rogers, Horace Wellington, and Henry Andrews, all Rockford young men, from boyhood. They have just completed a tour through the western states where they have received the ovation of professionals.

The Sons of Svea have also accomplished a commendable work in our midst, in the training of a large chorus of Swedish young men. They number sixty voices, under the directorship of Mr. Alfred Larson.

While too much cannot be said of these influences which have made Rockford audiences foremost among western cities for their appreciation of all that is highest and noblest in musical composition, yet we must not ignore still other elements which have recently entered into the musical fabric of our city.

Fitzgerald's Orchestra is the result of the careful selection of the best players our city affords, many of whom have devoted years to the study of orchestral music. Under their efficient and popular leader, Mr. F. A. Fitzgerald, this organization has become an indispensible quantity in our city. It comprises twenty-two pieces, and they are well equipped for the choice musical works introduced by their leader.

The Watch Factory Band, numbering thirty-five pieces, has more than a local reputation. With the influx of those who have been attracted by the business outlook of Rockford, we have been fortunate in numbering in this host many players from cities East and West, so that we now have in our band, musicians of experience, and their work is already rivaling that of older organizations. Mr. Fitzgerald is also leader of this band, and himself the master of the cornet. The Royal Sewing Machine Company's Band, Svea Band, Seventh Street Band, and Forest City Band are working in the same line, and each numbers from twelve to twenty members. Rockford presents no spasmodic growth of the musical elements which enter now so vitally into her existence, but side by side with her material progress and keeping pace with the educational and moral advancement has been the development of those principles which so certainly affect the taste and indicate the culture of a community.

It is not strange with all these things conspiring for the growth of our city that we apply the ancient proverb of Rome to our own community and claim that "Every road leads to Rockford."

Public School System.

THE educational advantages of Rockford are most excellent. The first school was established during the year 1839 in an old fashioned house built of logs on the east side of the river. In the same year another school was started on the west side. From this time on its citizens have taken the greatest interest in the public schools and other educational institutions, until now a diploma from the Rockford High School will admit the student to such institutions as Ann Arbor, Madison, Evanston, Beloit, and other colleges. Elsewhere these schools have been briefly alluded to, but they deserve a more emphatic notice. The Rockford public and parochial schools dispense their inestimable

DR. E. C. DUNN'S RESIDENCE.

A. D. FORBES' RESIDENCE.

blessings throughout our beautiful city. They act as an inspiration, for the irrepressible urchin of five or six years, delights in nothing so much as throwing away his infantile toys, abdicating this throne of "me big Injun," and with his satchel and shining face, marching like the soldier he has sometimes played himself to be, proudly to school. It is his first step to learning and manhood. The excellence of these schools of Rockford is surpassed nowhere, and are equalled in but few places. They are the pride of the people, the opportunities of the young. It is not to be expected, therefore, that these agencies should be permitted to languish, and they are not. No citizen, worthy of the name, begrudges the tax levied for their support. The official school census of Rockford, submitted June 30, 1890, showed 9,912 children between the ages of six and twenty-one. The city owns fourteen excellent school buildings and employs eighty competent school teachers. A list of the schools, cost of erection, etc., might not be out of place here.

THE HIGH SCHOOL. This building has the most approved sanitary arrangements, and all egresses open outward. It is in charge of Prof. Walter A. Edwards, a graduate of Knox College, assisted by a full corps of competent teachers. The cost of the building was about $50,000.

THE LINCOLN SCHOOL. A stone building, three stories in height. It is heated by steam and has a seating capacity of 450, and cost $30,000. It is in charge of Mary C. Spottswood as principal.

THE ADAMS SCHOOL. The building is a three-story stone structure, and has a seating capacity of 450 pupils. Its original cost was $30,000. This is in charge of Mary G. McPherson as principal.

THE HALL SCHOOL. Is a two-story stone building, and has a seating capacity of 350. The cost of this building was $12,000. The school is in charge of Miss Emma Coy as principal.

THE KENT SCHOOL. This is located in South Rockford, and is a stone building two stories high, and cost $25,000. Prof. O. F. Barbour is principal.

THE MARSH SCHOOL. This is a two story brick building, and accommodates 175 pupils. Cost, $8,000, and is in charge of Rose Cassidy.

THE KISHWAUKEE SCHOOL. Has a seating capacity of 200. The building cost $6,000, and is in charge of Matilda J. Nygren as principal.

THE MONTAGUE SCHOOL. Is a two-story brick building, and cost $12,000. Capacity 170. Elpha S. Moffatt is principal.

THE BLAKE SCHOOL. Cost, $6,000, and has a seating capacity of 150 pupils. Fanny Lyons is principal.

THE HASKELL SCHOOL. Cost $10,000, and has a seating capacity of 175. Anna Conaughy is principal.

THE ELLIS SCHOOL. Cost $7,000, and has a seating capacity of 160. Isabella M. Hunter is principal.

THE NELSON SCHOOL. Costing $10,000, and has a seating capacity of 175, and is now in charge of Mrs. Marie W. Rice as principal.

THE GARRISON SCHOOL. Has a seating capacity of 150, and cost $12,000. This school is in charge of Grace K. Crumb as principal.

THE WIGHT SCHOOL. Has just been completed at a cost of $25,000. This school is in charge of Mary C. Foote as principal.

Besides these there is an annex in charge of Jennie McAnarney.
Prof. P. R. Walker is general superintendent of city schools.

Rockford Seminary.

IN all the ages of the past, from the time the morning stars first sang together down to the present, there has never been a movement which had for its purpose the betterment of mankind but had its origin in woman's heart, and it was woman's hand that guided it to an end. There have been few movements of prominence of any kind but have had their principal chapters rendered more entrancing by the deeds or sayings of women. In all the names handed down by history, of the women rendered most famous, all are those whose minds were well stored with knowledge, and to-day, as in days gone by, it is the educated woman who is not only most highly prized but most useful as well.

Our excellent public schools of Rockford are worthy preparatory institutions, fitting our girls and boys to take their places in the world of battle, but it is to our higher institutions of learning that must be given the credit for the brightness which surrounds the names and lives of many of our people of the past and present. Probably there are none of the leading institutions of learning in our land that has given to society more bright ornaments in the way of cultured women than has the famous and justly famed Rockford Seminary. The Rockford Seminary is collegiate in character, and bears the title on account of the popularity of that title forty years ago, when the Seminary was founded. The location of the Seminary on high ground in East Rockford, commanding a full view of the pretty Forest City and the shining waters of the romantic Rock River, are such as to commend it as a health resort. The Seminary is not a denominational school, yet it is strictly a Christian school. Its buildings, as will be seen by engravings in another part of this book, are extensive brick buildings in the midst of a grove of oak and hickory trees, covering in all ten acres in extent. The Seminary is very popular, and numbers among its pupils each year students from all parts of the United States. One of the features which has done much to build up the popularity of the school with parents is the fact that the health of the pupils is carefully looked after. This is done by a comprehensive system of training in the gymnasium, run under the Sargent rules now in vogue in Harvard University. Frequent examinations are made and the health of the pupil is noted, and anything calculated to over-exert is forbidden. The home life of the school partakes more of the home than the ordinary boarding school, and is pleasant in all its features. The faculty of the Seminary has always been graced by the names of many of the country's leading educators, and to-day it is among the best in the land. Below will be found the Board of Trustees now in charge of this excellent school:

Board of Trustees—Prof. Joseph Emerson, D. D., President, Beloit, Wis.; G. A. Sanford, Esq., Vice-President, Rockford; Thomas D. Robertson, Esq., Treasurer, Rockford; Wm. A. Talcott., Esq., Secretary, Rockford.

Executive Committee—Hon. Wm. Lathrop, Chairman; Sarah F. Anderson, Secretary; Wm. A. Talcott, Esq., Mrs. Seely Perry, John Barnes, Esq., Henry H. Robinson, Esq.

The officers of government and instruction are: Sarah F. Anderson, Acting Principal and Financial Secretary; Jessie I. Spafford, B. A., Mathematics and Physical Science; Lena C. Leland, M. D., Resident Physician and Teacher in Physiology; Elizabeth Eastman, B. A., Rhetoric and Composition; Phebe T. Sutliff, M. A., History; Elizabeth L. Herrick, French Language and Literature; Alice A. Berry,

GOVERNMENT BUILDING, 1891-92.

Y. M. C. A. BUILDING.

B. A.. Greek and Latin; Florence Bascom, B. S., M. A., Chemistry and Natural Sciences; Alice L. Hulburd, B. A., History; Julia H. Gulliver, Ph. D., Philosophy; Anna C. Behrens, German Language and Literature; Lilian Jacoby, B. A., Drawing and Painting; Olive Rumsey. English Literature and Teacher of English; Effie Lunagan, Italian and Teacher of Latin: Anna H. Lathrop, B. A., Teacher of English; Elizabeth Ballard Thompson. B. A.. Teacher of Mathematics; Edith A. Sherman, Director of the Gymnasium; Emma G. Lumm, Teacher of Elocution; Mrs. Sarah E. Gregory, Matron; Marion I. Mead, Book-keeper and Librarian

Department of Music—Prof. Daniel N. Hood, Instrumental Music; Addie L. St. John, Vocal Music; Sarah Burton, Vocal Music; Mary R. Wilkins. B. A., Harmony.

Church Directory.

CENTENNIAL M. E. CHURCH. South Third Steeet. Rev. J. R. Hamilton, pastor. Property cost $60,000. Church has 600 members.

COURT STREET M. E. CHURCH. Corner Mulberry and Court Streets. Rev. W. A. Phillips, pastor. Rev. W. H. Haight, presiding elder Rockford district. Property valued at $100,000. Church will seat 2,200 persons, and has a membership of nearly 800.

GRACE M. E. CHURCH. Meets in Judd's Hall, West End. Rev. F. D. Sheets. pastor. Organized 1891 with one hundred members.

NINTH STREET M. E. CHURCH. Building new edifice on Ninth Street, to cost $10,000. Rev. J. F. Wardle, pastor. Has about 100 members.

WINNEBAGO STREET M. E CHURCH. Organized in 1864. Located in South Rockford. Rev. Henry Lea, pastor. Church property valued at $20,000. Has 300 members.

SWEDISH METHODIST CHURCH. Brick edifice, corner First Avenue and Fourth Street. Rev. A. A. Dahlberg, pastor.

FIRST BAPTIST CHURCH. Corner of Church and Mulberry Streets. Dr. C. H. Moscrip, pastor. Building erected in 1850. Property valued at $28,000. Church has 300 members.

STATE STREET BAPTIST CHURCH. Organized in 1858, and located at corner of State and Third Streets. Rev. J. T. Burhoe, pastor. Property valued at $35,000.

SWEDISH BAPTIST CHURCH. Brick edifice at corner of Seventh Street and Fourth Avenue. Rev. Petrus Swartz, pastor.

FIRST CONGREGATIONAL CHURCH Organized in 1837. Now located at corner of Kishwaukee Street and First Avenue. Rev. W. W. Leete, pastor Property valued at $60,000.

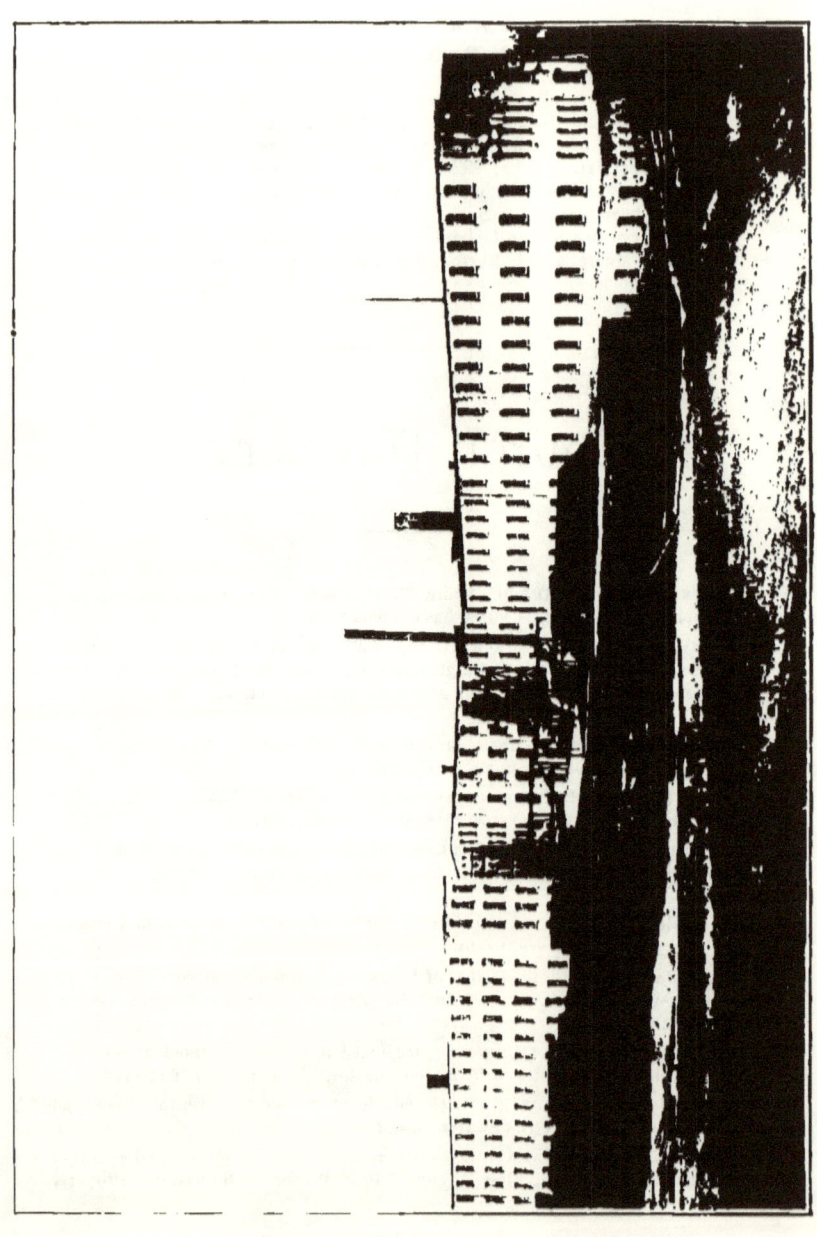

SECOND CONGREGATIONAL CHURCH. Organized 1849. New edifice at corner of Church and North Streets, to seat 2,000 persons. Dr. Walter M. Barrows, pastor. Value of all church property, $150,000.

LINCOLN MISSION. Colored. Meets in First Congregational Church Sunday afternoons.

FIRST LUTHERAN CHURCH. Organized 1854. Brick edifice at corner of Third and Oak. Largest Swedish church and congregation in the United States. Membership nearly 2,200. Rev. L. A. Johnston, pastor. Church property valued at $75,000.

ZION LUTHERAN CHURCH. Corner of First Avenue and Sixth Street. Present church built in 1885 at a cost of $30,000. Membership about 700. Rev. S. G. Ohman, pastor. Church building of brick and will seat 1,000 persons.

EMMANUEL GERMAN LUTHERAN CHURCH. Corner Third Avenue and Sixth Street. Rev. A. Fors, pastor. Edifice valued at $15,000, and will seat 800 persons.

FIRST LUTHERAN CHURCH. Corner of Chestnut and Church Streets. Rev. Prof. G. J. Kannmacher, pastor.

ST. PAUL'S GERMAN LUTHERAN CHURCH. Chestnut Street, between Church and Court. Brick edifice worth $10,000. Rev. L. W. Dorn, pastor.

FIRST PRESBYTERIAN CHURCH. North Main Street, near Mulberry. Church erected in 1868. Property valued at $60,000. Society organized in 1854. Rev. Geo. Harkness, pastor.

WESTMINSTER PRESBYTERIAN CHURCH. Organized in 1856. Brick church edifice, valued at $20,000; located at corner of Second and Oak Streets. Society has 300 members. Rev. W. M. Campbell, pastor.

CHURCH OF THE CHRISTIAN UNION. Undenominational. New edifice finished 1891, at a value of $60,000. Has 500 members. Dr. Thomas Kerr, pastor.

EMMANUEL EPISCOPAL CHURCH. Corner North and Church Streets. Dean D. C. Peabody, rector. Property valued at $25,000. Church has about 300 communicants.

ST JAMES CATHOLIC CHURCH. North Second Street. Rev. Fr. J. J. Flaherty, priest in charge. Have church building, school and deanery, valued at $75,000. There are about 800 parishioners.

ST. MARY'S CATHOLIC CHURCH. Corner of Winnebago and Elm Streets. Have one of the handsomest edifices in the city. Whole property valued at $85,000. Rev. Fr. M. L. McLaughlin, priest in charge; Father Wolff, assistant. There are about 2,500 parishioners on the roll. The church will seat nearly 1,500 persons.

SWEDISH MISSION TABERNACLE. Corner Kishwaukee Street and Third Avenue. Rev. F. M. Johnson, pastor. Church will seat 800 persons.

FIRST CHRISTIAN CHURCH. North First Street, between Market and Jefferson. Rev. H. M. Dennis, pastor. Church is of brick, will seat 400, and is valued at $8,000.

CALVARY UNION EVANGELICAL MISSION. Located on Kilburn Ave. Rev. T. J. Hunter, pastor.

SWEDISH FREE METHODIST CHURCH. Meets over 322 East State Street Rev. H. B. Marks, pastor.

BLAKEMAN & DOBSON CHURN FACTORY.

Z. B. STURTEVANT FLOUR MILL.

Her Health is Good.

EATH stalks through many communities in the form of an epidemic. Some cities have been ravaged by cholera, and others have been pillaged by grim yellow jack. Here lurks miasma and there the pestilence. Thrice happy, then, must be the spot so situated that no plague can reach it; where summer's sun and winter's chill are so tempered that suffering is unknown, and where the dry, clear breeze of the upland prairie bears health and energy on its wings. Much of the vigor of Rockford and Northern Illinois is due to the even and healthful climate she enjoys. The country is well above the lake level; there are no swamps or miasmatic spots, and the surface drainage is of the best. The average temperature is above sixty degrees, which scientists assert to be about the proper medium. There are no blizzards or extreme cold waves, and in summer the sun is seldom oppressive. The climate may well be described by the word genial. It is healthful, and the ravages of an epidemic are unknown. Rockford has the best and purest water to be found in the state. She has a perfect system of sewerage. She has an effective sanitary bureau and a complete method of house to house inspection. No pains or expense are spared to maintain her wonderful reputation as a healthy city. The death rate will not reach twelve per thousand a year, and her citizens can stay and attend to business through all seasons without experiencing discomfort. As a matter of fact Rockford might well advertise herself as a health resort, for there is certainly no city in the land that can make a better showing. She is in "the health belt," and her people are ruddy, vigorous, and full of sand.

Twenty Miles of Lumber

OTHING is a more convincing sign of the endurance and prosperity of a community than the erection of hundreds of handsome homes. They indicate plainer than words can do that the spot is one upon which the world has set the seal of approval. They deal with substance rather than shadow. It may be taken as a general rule that dwellings are not built unless there is someone to occupy them. The element of speculation is almost unknown in home building. Either a man builds for himself or else he pretty nearly knows who is to occupy the house he is constructing. Therefore, if eleven hundred new houses are built in one city within a twelve-month, it may be taken for granted that there is a growing and energetic municipality. Even during the winter months the good work was going on, and the visitor who drove over the city on last Christmas day would have found no less than two hundred and fifty residences in various stages of completion. Up in the North End additions there are one-hundred and twenty-five elegant homes where the corn was waving but little more than a year ago. In the West End a similar condition exists, and the factories

FOREST CITY KNITTING COMPANY. 1891.

SKANDIA PLOW COMPANY.

there are being surrounded by attractive dwellings. East and southeast have also been turned over to the builder and contractor, and many of the finest residences in the city are there to be found. The lumber used in a season's building operations in Rockford exceeded 40,000,000 feet, and would make a railroad train more than twenty miles long. Most of this went into house building, and when the stores and factories are added to the list the season's work will exceed $1,500,000. The present season promises to be even greater, as several very expensive buildings are to be included in the list. It will be but a little time before Rockford will be one of the best built cities in the west. Four to six-story buildings are becoming the rule, and the residences will compare with those of any city in the land. A thousand more new houses will be built within another year, and still it will be found difficult to find a place to lay the head. There are no vacant stores or dwellings in the city to-day, and small prospect of there being any for some time to come. House building is a certain investment, and with the judicious purchase of real estate can be made to yield a profit of ten to twenty-five per cent. the first year. The men who build houses in Rockford are taking no chances. They are backing a sure thing. There's no such word as fail.

Uncle Sam's Business.

THE postage stamp gets thoroughly licked in Rockford and the business transacted in Uncle Sam's office is very extensive. The reports of the Postmaster General upon the affairs of the 128 first-class offices in the land, show that Rockford stands far higher than her population would warrant. She ranks with cities of 40,000 or 50,000 population. There is no better criterion of a city's enterprise and commercial standing than these self-same post-office statements. The last report shows that the receipts of the office are over $55,000 a year. The per cent. of increase over the previous year's business is thirteen, which is just the same as the advance in Chicago and greater than any other city in the state. Take, in fact, all statistics—postal, railroad, financial and otherwise, and they clearly show that Rockford is the second city in the great state of Illinois. It takes a Chicago to beat her. The manufactories, the insurance companies, the seed farms, and the real estate interests all aid in swelling the purse of Uncle Sam, who makes an annual net profit of over $30,000 out of the Forest City. Col. Thomas G. Lawler is the efficient postmaster. He has eight office assistants and fourteen carriers. Two more carriers are needed and will be allowed. There are sixty street boxes. The carriers handle over 6,000,000 pieces of mail matter each year, and do it with smiling faces. So important has the postal business of Rockford become that the last congress appropriated $100,000 for the erection of a suitable government building, and elaborate plans have already been prepared for the structure, work upon the foundation of which is already undertaken. It will be an edifice in which the citizens may take justifiable pride.

ILLINOIS CHAIR COMPANY. 1891.

HESS & HOPKINS' TANNERY.

Winnebago County.

— — —

ILLINOIS was admitted into the union of states in April 1818, and at that time
its population was but a trifle larger than Rockford boasts of to-day. What is
now Winnebago county was visited by white people in 1832 and 1833. The
first white settler, however, is generally reputed to have been Stephen Mack,
who pitched his cabin near the mouth of the Pecatonica river, about twelve
miles north of the Rockford of the present day, some time about 1829. Stephen
was a college graduate, a Vermonter, and something of a dude, but for some reason
he drifted west into the fur business, married a squaw and became the patron
saint of Winnebago county. In after years when the ford had become Rockford
and a seminary had been reared, two of his daughters attended school there for a
time. But their wild Indian blood rebelled and they soon drifted away to the reser-
vation in Minnesota.

John Phelps cruised down the Pecatonica from Mineral Point, Wis , in 1833,
and landed where South Rockford now spreads herself. He stopped but a short
time, however, but took to his canoe again and journeyed down to start the town of
Oregon. In the mouth of August of the following year Germanicus Kent of Ala-
bama and Thatcher Blake of Maine came down from Galena by wagon and boat
and struck the same South Rockford spot. There they settled and Kent built a
saw mill, near the mouth of what is now Kent's creek. Both pioneers are now
dead, but Mrs. Thatcher Blake still lives in a handsome home on a portion of the
beautiful farm her husband claimed on the bank of Rock river, just south of the
city limits. After the arrival of these settlers the country began to receive numerous sturdy pioneers. They came mainly from the New England States. In June
1835 the population of the Rockford settlement was eleven souls and a like number
of bodies. In January 1836, the county of Winnebago was organized, then including what is now the county of Boone. In August 1836, the first election was held,
and 120 votes were cast. Winnebago county was in 1840 set apart to its present
size. Now it is one of the greatest counties in a great state. It contains 50,000
busy people, and for manufacturing and agriculture casts down its gauntlet to the
entire nation. The farming districts are wealthy and teem with the best products of
the soil. Nature intended Winnebago to be a magnificent and prosperous area, and
the results have not belied her wishes.

The affairs of the county have ever been administered with fidelity and wisdom. She has always been well governed. The most imposing court house in Illinois outside of Chicago was built here at a cost of $250,000. All the buildings,
bridges, and improvements owned by the county are of the very best, and in deed
and truth she blossoms as the rose. The leading county officials at the present
time are:—

County Judge—Rufus C. Bailey.
County Clerk—Marcus A. Norton.
Circuit Clerk—Lewis F. Lake.
Sheriff—Joel Burbank.
County Treasurer—John Beatson.
State's Attorney—Chas. A. Works.
Supt. of Schools—Chas. J. Kinnie.
Coroner—N. S. Aagesen.
Master-in-Chancery—H. W. Taylor.

RHOADES-UTTER PAPER MILL.

GEO. F. PENFIELD'S RESIDENCE.

Real Estate in Rockford.

EAL ESTATE is the basis of all values, the foundation of all investments. From the dawn of time to the tail end of eternity it was and must be considered the chief factor in the world's material advancement. Columbus was looking for real estate when he sailed westward and discovered a new hemisphere. Those Spanish adventurers of three and four hundred years ago were all real estate prospectors and speculators. It is true they wanted mines of gold and silver thrown in, but still they did not fail to raise the royal standard and claim the real estate in the name of the king. Conquest is but another name for transfering realty. Alexander was the greatest landholder of his time, and he died crying because there were not more additions he might open. This passion for land acquirement has been the means of bearing civilization into many a dark corner of the earth. The pioneer and the explorer have made this world the desirable place of residence it is. The sturdy sons of New England wandered forth into the west, and lo! the Mississippi valley blossomed as the rose. They saw that the land was fair and so they possessed it. It is to their wisdom and forethought; their ambition for real estate possession, that Rockford to-day owes her prosperity. Those enterprising settlers have made corner lots valuable, and caused Rockford realty to become good as gold. They live to see the fruition of their hopes, and as the city spreads they smile.

The development of Rockford is in no one direction. The railroads so surround it that all parts possess equal advantages. They build side tracks wherever asked, and all factories are placed upon equal footing so far as railway and shipping facilities are concerned. Thus it has been that Rockford has quietly spread herself in all directions. The North End, the West End, the East Side, and the South Side have all swelled without detriment to one another. A dozen sub-divisions have been opened up, and each one has demonstrated the need of the community for it. No wild western methods are needed to float Rockford real estate. The newer additions contain no less than twenty of the largest factories in the city. The employes in nearly every instance are heads of families, and what is more natural than that they should desire a home near where they are employed? The result is that clean, cozy and cheerful manufacturing additions surround the city, and real estate is everywhere enhanced in value. It is a matter of record that a dollar was never lost in an investment in Rockford realty, and that many persons have made snug fortunes with but little capital to start with. The advance in values has been rapid, but well sustained. The rule of supply and demand is made to apply to the real estate business. There is no unnatural forcing of property upon the market. Men who build homes and intend to occupy them themselves are permitted to buy lots at bed-rock prices, and are also given financial assistance as the work of construction goes on. There is no speculation in real estate circles. No man is taking any chances or running any risk when he puts money in land in the Forest City. Prices are not up in the skies. Desirable lots in the best manufacturing and residence additions can be had for from $200 to $800. They are invariably 50x150 feet in size, and are easily accessible by one of the numerous rapid electric car lines. Along the river are some of the handsomest residence sites imaginable, and these sub-divisions are being built up with a very superior class of homes. Values are correspondingly higher, and the purchaser willingly pays $1,200 to $2,000 for his bargain. Highland, Sunrise. Churchill Place. and other East Side additions are also purely residence sub-divisions, and being well built up. The other additions contain more or less manufacturing, and property has a perma-

COMMERCIAL CLUB (INTERIOR) 1891.

nent and known value. In the southeast part of the city a remarkable development in this respect is noted.

Property in the business portion of the heart of the city is held at well advanced prices, but in all other directions there is no attempt to crowd values. Realty at the junction of the two principal streets of the city cannot be touched for $1,500 a foot, although the lots are but seventy feet deep, and this, too, without taking the buildings into consideration. Property on Main and State streets, in the commercial center, ranges from $250 to $1,000 per foot. These values have been maintained for several years, and clearly indicate the permanence and stability of a Rockford investment. Two years ago a syndicate sought to secure a site on West State street on which to erect a huge office building. They tramped from one end to the other and could find no one who desired to sell. The office building is now erected on another street where a vacant site was found. The old city—the Rockford of ten years ago—is well built up. Very little of it is for sale, and that by parties who desire to build and dwell in the newer, out-lying portions, which are made central and accessible by rapid electric railway lines. The development of these additions has been remarkable. The class of residences erected are superior in their average to those in the more central part of the city. The lots were purchased for one-third or one-half the prices of the others, and yet the resident can reach his store or office in less time than his down-town friend. He rides; the other walks. For the thousands who are employed in the factories, and who are in most instances heads of families, the land surrounding these industrial institutions is in great demand. They want homes, and they are enabled to purchase lots at very reasonable figures. Many shrewd investors are putting up large numbers of dwellings, and are renting or selling them so as to net a handsome profit. There is room for more of these. The demand for houses is far greater than the supply. The enterprising men interested in the development of these newer residence districts have put in at least a million dollars of their own money, and have laid a sure foundation. They offer fair and square propositions to capitalist and workingman alike. Lots for actual home builders may be bought at very low figures, with an absolute certainty of their being a profitable investment. Rockford people invest their savings in Rockford realty. They realize that they are taking no chances then.

The Bridges.

B EAUTIFUL Rock River winds through Rockford, and divides it into two districts almost equal in population. Six costly bridges span this stream, and trade and commerce goes back and forth upon them. They represent an outlay of $250,000 on the part of the city and the railroads. It has been the policy of the municipality to build well. The steel plate girder bridge at State street, which was put in last year, cost the city over $60,000, and is said to be the strongest and best constructed road bridge in the United States. It was completed early in 1891 by the contractors, the Massillon Bridge Company, of Massillon, Ohio. The bridge is about five hundred feet in length, and stands on four stone piers, with massive abutments on either bank. It is a superb specimen of bridge construction in its every detail. There are also twenty excellent bridges across Kent's and Keith's Creeks, most of them built of iron, and the massive Winnebago street viaduct, spanning the entire yards of C., M. & St. P., C., B. & Q.. and I. C. railroads.

ILLINOIS CENTRAL DEPOT AND GROUNDS.

Rockford's Clearing House.

TO say that the financial and fiduciary interests of the Forest City at the present time are of surpassing importance, does not adequately convey an idea of the extent thereof. The vast amount of capital invested in banking and kindred lines, and the altogether phenomenal increase in savings and deposits in our many and varied moneyed institutions during the past few years, have given Rockford supremacy as the financial centre in Northern Illinois outside of Chicago, and all the indications are that she is bound to maintain the lead in this respect. In no city of its size can a like number of solid and substantial corporations be found whose career has been uninterrupted prosperity; passing through seasons of panic, business depressions, and stringency in the money market with credit and usefulness unimpaired and standing and stability unshaken, as have the banks of this city. The vast amount of business done by the several banks has made it absolutely necessary for a clearing house, and such steps were taken a short time ago. Rockford has a very large business, and in all probability will be able to show daily clearings of $150,000 to $200,000 per day. It has been customary for the messenger boys from each bank to visit all the other banks with the checks each day for a settlement, but under the present system it has been simplified, until the time required to transact all the business is but thirty minutes instead of half a day as formerly.

The West End Observatory.

NONE of the loftiest elevations in or around Rockford—lying just west of the base ball park, is soon to be erected the "West End Observatory," which will prove one of the most novel attractions that any city can boast of. It is not a tower of Babel, although it seems much akin to it. It will tower toward the skies like one of the pyramids, or like the sculptured shaft of Cleopatra's needle. A stock company has been formed for its construction and the projectors look upon it as an excellent investment. Its location is in the heart of the flourishing West End addition, on the line of the new electric railway, thus furnishing an attraction calculated to bring wealth into the coffers of the street car company. The plans call for a tower forty feet square, rising to an altitude of nearly two hundred feet. There will be a steam power elevator to carry visitors quickly to the top. There a broad panorama will be unfolded to the eye and a perfect view of the Forest City and its beauties be presented. There will be landings at various stages of the journey. Refreshment booths will be maintained, and concerts will be given at the observatory from time to time. It will also be an excellent spot for pyrotechnic displays.

E. W. BLAISDELL'S RESIDENCE.

JOHN BARNES' RESIDENCE.

Before and After the War.

THE good old county of Winnebago sent forth 3,200 brave men during the civil war period. The county was not as populous then as now, and they could not well be spared. But they respected their country's call and went just the same. It was in Rockford that the nucleus of the Ellsworth Zouaves was formed, and many a gallant leader hailed from Winnebago county. The Illinois department of the Grand Army of the Republic is the senior body in that organization. Col. Nevius Post, of Rockford, is Post No. 1 of that department, and therefore leader in national demonstrations of the order. Col. Thos. G. Lawler has been commander of the post since its organization, twenty-three years ago. There are still over five hundred surviving members. They have extensive auxiliaries, too, in the Woman's Relief Corps, and a camp of Sons of Veterans.

The militia of to-day is also well represented in Rockford. The city is the headquarters of the Third Regiment Illinois National Guard, and two companies are located here. In local parlance they are known as the Rockford Rifles and the Rockford Grays. The latter are the progenitors of the Ellsworth Zouaves, but the former has become the senior company by reason of the reorganization of the other. The regiment is commanded by Col. Thos. G. Lawler. Other regimental officers in Rockford are: Adjutant, Lewis F. Lake; Chaplain, G. R. Vanhorne; Inspector of Rifle Practice, P. T. Anderson. Capt. Wm. Wildt leads the Grays to victory or defeat, and Capt. A. E. Fisher heads the Rifles.

A Complete Sewer System.

WITHOUT good drainage, sanitary plumbing and the exercise of ordinary health methods, any community is apt to be threatened with disease. Rockford fears nothing. She is well situated, and boasts of one of the most perfect sewer systems in the state. A broad river flows through her center, almost evenly dividing the population, and on either side two creeks trace their way through much of each division, furnishing natural water courses. The sewer system as carried out follows the work of nature very closely. Through these valleys large mains have been placed and auxiliary sewers drain into these as well as directly into the river. It is the opinion of the leading engineers of the time that the Rockford system is one of the best in the country and will provide for the future. At present it is as complete as will usually be found in a city of 50,000 people. About four miles of new mains are laid each year. The system, when this season's operations are concluded, will embrace about twenty-one miles, representing an outlay of nearly $200,000. The sewer department is quite an important one in the city. All plumbing must be done by licensed plumbers, and the connections are all subject to city examination and approval. There is a liberal supply of catch basins and manholes, and the mains are all of ample size to perform their mission of cleansing a beautiful city.

ROCKFORD PLOW COMPANY.

Rockford's Paved Streets.

CLEAN, well-kept and well-paved thoroughfares are a very reliable indication of the spirit of enterprise that prevails in a municipality. Nothing impresses a stranger more in visiting a city than to find that the streets are smooth and well cared for. Rockford has an excellent pavement system which is being constantly enlarged. Experiments have been made with cedar blocks, brick and granite as paving materials, and the two former are in use. The first pavement laid in Rockford was that of East State Street, which was completed in the fall of 1889. Since that time much more has been laid, and this year will witness the doubling of the paving area. All the central business portion of the city is now paved, as also are the two leading residence thoroughfares. Ordinances are prepared for the paving of other streets, and the present plan of the pavement system includes over fifty blocks which will cost when all completed nearly $300,000. Much of this pavement was laid by local contractors. It is all of the best and is invariably clean and well cared for. It affords superb surface drainage in the business portion and the thoroughfares are usually as neat as a New England kitchen. It is indeed one of Rockford's boasts that she is a well paved city. The paving contracts awarded alone in the month of June 1891 exceeded $92,000, and several others were then still pending.

Addenda and Errata.

The directory of industries and corporations, commencing on page 27 has received some additions since its compilement. June 1891 was a busy month among men of enterprise. Some changes are also to be recorded in established institutions, so that this chapter of addenda and errata is made necessary:

Graham Brothers. This corporation, which operates woolen, cotton and paper mills, and also two distilleries, have purchased the large Keeney paper mill plant on the east bank of Rock river, and have made extensive additions and alterations. They have invested $75,000 in the business and will run night and day. They employ forty hands in the paper mill; turn out a product of $150,000 per annum, and their pay roll is about $22,000 a year.

American Burial Case Company. Incorporated July 1891. Capital $30,000. Organized by Emil Youngberg and Karl V. Berglund. Will probably erect a four-story brick and frame building in Robertson's Stockholm Park addition, east of Churchill Place. Will employ fifty hands, with an annual business of $75,000 and a pay-roll of $22,000. The company expects to increase its capital to $50,000 within a few months.

Rockford Flour Sieve Company. Incorporated July 1891, by Dr. John Thelberg, H. Wallerstedt, R. G. McEvoy, and others. Capital $25,000. Plant not yet located. Will employ twenty hands and expect to do a business of $25,000 a year.

Champion Watch Company. Organized July 1891, by L. E. Crandall, Matthias Bredt, S. E. Mayo and others. Capital stock $250,000. The company expect to build in Manning's addition in the West End. Their factory will be of brick, 60x250 feet in size and two stories high. They will do a business of $100,000 a year and expect to exploy 200 hands, with a pay-roll of $120,000 per annum.

Rock River Planing Mill Company. Organized July 1891, with a capital of $50,000.

Fidelity Building and Loan Association. Organized May and June 1891. Authorized capital $20,000,000. George M. Blake, President; Gilbert Woodruff, Vice-President; Wm. G. Bennett, Secretary; Will F. Woodruff, Treasurer.

Rockford Improvement Association. E. M. Revell, President; Geo. F. Penfield, Secretary. The interests of the city looked after, and all information furnished inquirers. Factory sites located.

West End Improvement Company. B. A. Knight, General Manager. To develop all West End property.

H. W. Price Improvement Company. H. W. Price, President; E. H. Marsh, Secretary. Organized to build up and improve North End property.

Harlem Park Company. Organized 1891. Capital $5,000. E. H. Marsh, President; John H. Camlin, Secretary.

DRAWINGS PROPOSED BY▢▢ · "HOTEL NELSON. D. S. SCHUREMAN, ARCHITECT.

Rockford Sugar Works. Located between Seminary Street and Rock river. B. J. Musser, President; Edward J. Holden, Secretary. Capital $300,000. Occupy three large buildings, four and five stories high. Employ from fifty to three hundred hands, and do a business of $500,000 a year.

Mechanics' Machine Company. Capital, $10,000. Organized by Levin Faust, Gustaf A. Dalin and Carl J. Forsberg. Do a general machine shop business.

Climax Slide and Table Company. W. I. Weld succeeds L. B. Garrett as secretary.

Royal Sewing Machine Company. W. H. Dugdale is made general superintendent.

West End Furniture Company. Mr. J. H. Lynn has been elected secretary. The company purposes to double the size of its plant in a short time.

Star Furniture Company. Secretary P. G. Lundquist being on the road much of the time. Emil Swenson has been elected assistant secretary.

Who Did the Work.

THE engravings in this work are all half-tone cuts made by A. Zeese & Co., of Chicago. Nearly all were taken from photographs by Erick Erickson. The printing and binding is the work of the Forest City Publishing Company. We are indebted to Mr. D. S. Schureman, the Architect, for drawings furnished for the following buildings: The Forest City Knitting Co., Oscar Nelson's Residence, Ingersoll Milling Machine Co., Frank Barnes' Flats, Second Congregational Church, and the Hotel Nelson.

DIAMOND FURNITURE COMPANY—1891.

A. HIME BARREL FACTORY.

WILLIAM BROWN BUILDING.

MRS. S. C. MILLER'S RESIDENCE. (HIGHLAND ADDITION.)

www.ingramcontent.com/pod-product-compliance
Lightning Source LLC
Chambersburg PA
CBHW020755020726
47495CB00008B/2444